The Last Good Man

The Last Good Man

Patience Swift

BEAUTIFULBOOKS

First published 2006
This edition published 2008

Beautiful Books Limited
36-38 Glasshouse Street
London W1B 5DL

www.beautiful-books.co.uk

ISBN: 9781905636297

9 8 7 6 5 4 3 2 1

A catalogue reference for this book is available
from the British Library.

Jacket design by Head Design
Printed and bound in the UK by CPI Mackays, Chatham ME5 8TD

Acknowledgements:

The author and publishers would like to thank Penguin Books Ltd
for permission to quote from The Letters of Abelard and Heloise,
translated by Betty Radice (Penguin Classics, 1974).
Copyright © Betty Radice, 1974.

One

'Not right. Not thinking right. Dead. Dead very soon.'

Now here he is: Sam. He's such a massive man, he stands four or five inches taller than the crowd around him. He's huge. The crowd of villagers and tourists, about sixty or seventy of them, are gathered around the railings overlooking the beach. The curve of the bay reaches out to the left and right and joins at the horizon with a line of blue about a mile long, and now the bowl of water enclosed by the bay and ending here at the beach is roaring and frothing with the competing cross-currents and the waves are already breaking four or five hundred yards out.

There's a couple standing close to him. They are wearing colourful clothes, the ones you buy in the shop back home when you are preparing for your holiday. They are frowning at Sam, this big man. His words are inappropriate. Beside them stands a woman, holding the handle of a suitcase. She has dense, long blonde hair, and she has turned her gaze from the sea towards Sam.

There's someone dying out in the bay. He is being watched by this crowd on the beach. They urge each other on: 'He can make it, I can see him, he can make it,' and 'The kiddies are safe!' and 'Look, he's still swimming!' They nod to each other, stare at each other imploringly. Some say prayers out loud. The emotion heaves through them clumsily.

Sam's words aren't right.

He moves on, his gaze not specific. He should not have spoken aloud, he knows that. Just move on now, he thinks. Go quietly. He knows these situations, and although he never fully understands why, he knows that a crowd like this is not willing to be truthful.

The man, a tourist it seems, had been swept out by the rip tide trying to reach his two children – their rubber dinghy had been pulled out into the centre of the bay. Sam had seen immediately that he was going to die. When two strong currents meet each other in a powerful sea, they can create a rip, and the energy created by the rip can drive anything in its path out into the deeper water where the breaking waves will pound and pound. The children in the boat will survive – the waves aren't huge, and as long as they stay in the boat, they will be picked up by the coastguards soon. But their father is swimming, and he is frantically, hysterically smashing arms and legs into wave after wave, trying to fight the force of the rip.

Sam had seen it before. He had been caught in rips himself, and knew that they were not dangerous if you showed them respect. Just swim gently, let the rip take you, keep quiet. In half an hour, forty minutes, you'd be half a mile away, in stiller water, and you could swim slowly to the shore, a long way from the village by then. Never fight it.

He smiles. Fancy trying to fight an ocean! A man, and he tries to fight an ocean! Well, he can try, but he'd never seen anyone last more than twenty minutes. The man would be dead very soon.

He walks past the end of the crowd, notes the lifeboat being pushed into the crashing waves on the shore but keeps looking ahead, his face calm, his mouth kindly, his eyes looking quietly into the distance. He walks slowly, his big solid hands each cradling the handles of carrier bags which hold the provisions he has just bought from the village grocery. The handles of the bags barely make an impression on his woody fingers. The long, neat acrylic blue trousers he pressed with an iron yesterday, and into them is tucked a faded yellow short sleeve shirt. The steps he makes are regular, and the navy beach shoes make no sound as he walks. Sam has thick, sandy hair that once had been ginger but at fifty seven it has still not begun to recede.

At the end of the little seafront promenade, where the railings finish at the steps which lead down to the beach, and the road continues on past the last few shops and cafés up towards the steep hill leading out of the village, he sees a boy, perhaps eight or nine, sitting on a bicycle. The boy looks tired and unhappy, and his face is red. It is a hot day, the sun is very bright. The boy is upset. The chain of his bike is clattering badly against the gearing cogs and the bicycle stands still. Sam pauses beside the boy, not looking straight at him but diagonally, at an angle as he has learned to do over the years and years of his life, so that he can see but not be drawn in.

He carefully rests the two carrier bags down on the pavement, and bends his knees so that he is crouching, eyes level with the seat of the bicycle.

'You're not supposed to be there,' he says, not to the boy, but to the oily black bicycle chain, and he gently pokes his thick first finger under the caught chain, stretches it upwards so that the sprockets spring clear of the cog, and then he replaces it once more, this time fitting the sprockets into each tooth, pulling the chain around the cog as he goes.

'You won't work like that,' he smiles, 'making all that commotion. Want to be easy, take each tooth, fit it in. Much better.'

He tugs at the chain guard, which has twisted causing the chain to miss its path, and then he stands up. The boy is staring at him, he doesn't say anything. Sam picks some leaves from the low hedge that runs at the foot of the railings and wipes the black oil from his fingers. The boy suddenly pushes down on his pedal and the chain grips and he races off back towards the crowd.

Sam picks up his bags and continues to walk, slowly and calmly, up the increasing gradient of the road that climbs out of the village. The noise of the surf on the beach grows quieter in the hot sunshine as he climbs higher and higher up the long hill, and out in the middle of the bay the man feels the last strength in his arms disappear into the violent water and he gulps one final whole mouthful of seawater and he drowns.

Standing on the seafront, Isobel watched the man die.

The noise around her was ugly. There were frantic screams coming from a group down on the sand, and Isobel thought this must be part of the family. The crowd around her were moaning and calling out now – 'I can't see him any more! I can't see him!' – and some voices were becoming angry, emotional. A man yelled: 'Why didn't they do something? Why was the lifeboat out so late?'

Isobel looked at him. He was red in the face, with sweat licking at the hair on his brow. She thought: I am sorry for him; he doesn't want to accept it, not like the man who had passed by them earlier. He had said something odd, she thought: something about not thinking. No, the man beside her now didn't want it to be happening, and in fact he was crying now. A woman put her arm around his shoulder, and he turned his head into her, weeping.

Ah, how can this be? Isobel felt very tired suddenly, and she realised she was still clutching the handle of her suitcase. She let go, and sat down on the rim of the case. She put her hands on her knees, and let her head drop.

Somehow the noise seemed greater now: the crying, the talking, the beating of the surf, and here in the background the wail of an ambulance. She felt the heat again, and the stickiness of her clothes after the long journey.

She breathed slowly and deeply, and shut her eyes. She had learned about breathing recently, how to inflate your lungs calmly and open your chest to fill them. Then when you exhale, you push the air out through a little gap between your lips very quietly and slowly, and you keep pushing until your muscles below your lungs have emptied them. When she learned this, at a class back in the city last year, she was taught to think of a wave on a beach after it had broken, and to think of her exhaling breath as though it were the seawater flooding up the beach, still pushing and pushing further up the beach until the last energy of the wave is used up. Then the slightest of pauses, when the water on the beach looks completely still, and then the sea draws back once more and you begin to breathe in again.

Isobel sat like this for a minute or two. She opened her eyes and lifted up her head. Out in the bay she could see the lifeboat circling and the crew looking down into the sea, but it was rough out there and the boat was thrown about by the swell and the waves.

She had asked the taxi to drop her at the seafront only fifteen minutes ago. She was going to go straight to the hotel, but she had wanted to see why the crowds were gathered. It's a normal instinct, isn't it, to be drawn to the crowd? Then she had found out what was happening. She had seen people die before, and it was that which had suddenly exhausted her: it was familiar, all this emotion and bewilderment and fear. She had seen it before, time and again, as the curtains were drawn around a bed on the ward. Now here, again, in the village where she grew up.

It is not how she had imagined returning home after ten years.

Sam had reached the top of the hill now. The road from the village which he had been climbing levels out at about two hundred feet above the sea, and it swings off to the right at the point where the coast path begins. There was a walkers' guiding sign pointing down the path, and a thick wooden seat with a tarnished brass plate sunk into the middle of it with the words *For Angie, for she did love this view so.*

He placed his bags beside one of the stone seat supports and sat down, conscious that he was still breathing through his nose; one of the things which Sam worried about was physical decline, and he feared the time when he would have to open his mouth to seize more oxygen after the climb up the hill.

Not yet, he thought, and he nodded. Still strong.

From the seat you could see over the roofs of the village below. The buildings were huddled around the

curve of the beach, perhaps three hundred or so buildings, and from up here Sam could see the alleyways
which connected the few streets which ran back from the
promenade. He looked down the steep hill he had just
walked up, over the roofs and the streets, and over to the
long white building set into the cliffs on the other side
of the village. This was the hotel where most of the holidaymakers stayed. In the winter of course it was mostly
empty, but now in August there were all the signs of occu-
pation: towels hanging out of windows, umbrellas and
tables laid out on the gravel at the front of the building.
Framed in an open window, a wetsuit swayed black in
the breeze, dangling from a hanger on a veranda.

Further to the east of the hotel, the cliffs became wild
again up to the point of the headland, and Sam's gaze
continued across the line of the horizon to the western
headland, and back along the curve of the bay up to his
vantage point.

He liked this position. He enjoyed the seat: it was well
made, he'd guess about three inches, three and a half
inches of maple. It had been put up a few years ago when
the last one rotted away. He remembered there always
being a seat here at the start of the coast path, even when
he was a boy and he was racing back home after school,
running along the path to find his mother with hot tea
ready and a piece of bread with her damson jam smeared
on it, the tea set out on the table and her standing by the
window with a beautiful smile to hide the tiredness she

felt from another day cleaning for houses in the village.

Sam looked down along the line of the cliff, focussing carefully on each outcrop of rock.

'There he is,' he said, smiling again. 'Look out beetles, look out mice, he's here.'

Down below, a peregrine falcon extended its wings and lifted itself up from an edge, then swept over the heather and gorse of the cliff, gliding ten or fifteen feet over the ground to settle again on another rock jutting out of the red brown cliff face. The noise of the surf down below in the village was like a whisper, and the sun was high overhead now so that Sam could feel the heat of it working through the fibres of his shirt about his shoulders. High above him a starling suddenly sang.

'No good just sitting here,' Sam said. 'Work won't do itself, Sam.'

He stood up, bent down to pick up his two bags again and began to walk along the rough coast path that took him away from the road and into the headland. The path was wide – four, four and a half feet perhaps if he measured it by stretching his huge arms out from one side to the other – but after he had been walking along it for five minutes he turned right and began to climb again up a narrower path closely bordered by thick hedges of brambles.

Sometimes he didn't take this more difficult way but would continue on the coast path all the way around the headland, past the lighthouse at the tip, to his house which lay on the other side. But today he knew he should be home earlier while the sun was still strong so that he could varnish the wood of the new cladding he had applied to the north side of the house.

They always called this steep path the 'cut-through' when he was growing up, and it took you up another hundred feet over the brow of the headland so that at the top you got a view of the village and its bay to the east, the headland and the lighthouse due south, and to the west the huge spread of the next bay, probably four miles of clean sand and rock and sea, which had for Sam provided the backdrop to his whole life.

'It's over, they've found him.'

The lifeguards had radioed back to shore, and the crowd understood that they had not been in time to save the poor soul. There was more sobbing now, and the man beside Isobel renewed his choking cry, his wife patting him absent-mindedly on the shoulder as he wept. His continued reaction irked Isobel – she could see he was not a relative, you could always tell the relatives: they stayed quiet at the end. Why take on so?

She stood up. She should move on up to the hotel now. She had left the city soon after dawn this morning and had been on the train for hours. She would like to settle in to her hotel before she had to talk to anyone.

She extended the handle and walked on down the

seafront promenade away from the crowd, her suitcase trundling behind her on its plastic wheels. The sun was high now, and her long, thick hair glowed like bronze as it flowed down her back. She wore jeans, a cotton shirt, and her skin was brown from sessions at the sunbed back in the city. She didn't wear make up, and two men running down below on the beach towards the crowds looked up at her as she passed.

Isobel didn't notice them. She scanned the little shops and cafés along the seafront road ahead of her. Everything seemed tiny, which is how it always is when you return to where you lived as a child. She couldn't recognise the shops, and the café with its tables scattered outside on the pavement seemed brash and new. She walked on, not conscious now of the churning sea on her right, wondering whether at the end of the row the little bookshop would still be there. It was always the last shop in the row, she was sure of that: the tiny second-hand bookshop with the dark, musty interior. Where she had spent so much time, so many years ago.

Of course, it wasn't there. As she turned the corner to begin the climb up the slope towards the hotel at the end of the village, the last shop was an off-licence. In the doorway stood a young man, no older than Isobel had been when she left home. She smiled, but he was looking out beyond her towards the sea.

She stopped in front of him.

'Hello,' she said. 'I haven't been here for such a long

time. Do you happen to know, was this shop a bookshop once?'

The boy turned to look at her, frowning.

'What?'

'A bookshop. Was your shop a bookshop once, do you know?'

He frowned more, his lip curling up. 'It's an off licence. Drink.'

'Yes, I can see that. I was just –'

'Can't you see what's happening out there?' he snapped. 'You want to buy a book, and there's some poor bloke drowning out there.' He shook his head, and walked back into the shop, the bell on top of the door jangling.

She walked on, pulling her clattering suitcase.

That's all right. She understood. He was probably right.

Only it would have been nice, to have seen the old bookshop. When she was at school here in the village, twenty years ago now, she worked on Saturdays for the old man who owned the shop, arranging the books on the shelves, setting them straight and neat with a concern for precision which always amused him.

Isobel knew that the intensity of her feelings when she worked in that shop had stayed with her all her life. While the old man dozed in the back room, she sat beside the till at the counter in the bookish silence with the dust particles twisting in the shafts of sunlight coming through the dirty windows, and she read and read. Her parents thought it a 'good thing' that she earned herself pocket money, but they never asked her about the books, and she was always relieved about that. Even back then, she couldn't bear to have to talk about the books she read, the thoughts they inspired.

She was no different now, she thought. It would have been nice if the shop had been there. She could have stepped back into it, taken a book from the shelf, sat at the desk and begun to read in the silence.

She began to climb the short slope that led from the end of the promenade up to the hotel. As she reached the top, she thought of Héloise. It was in the shop that she had first read about Héloise.

'I moderate what it is difficult or rather impossible to forestall in speech. For nothing is less under our control than the heart – having no power to command it we are forced to obey. And so when its impulses move us, none of us can stop their sudden promptings from easily breaking out, and even more easily overflowing into words which are the every-ready indications of the heart's emotions.'

Isobel went into the hotel, intense in her heart's emotions.

From the brow of the hill the narrow stony path begins to descend again, and Sam could see his house now fifty yards away, the whitewashed stone wall around it making a bright line against the green and brown leaves of the hillside.

The house had been built by his great-grandfather in the late nineteenth century. He had been an entrepreneurial man who had carried stone and mortar and lead and copper pipes and glass over the brow of the headland from the village to build a house on the cliffs overlooking the great bay which could host an oil-burning light to warn ships off the reefs. In return for his back-breaking effort and initiative, Sam's great-grandfather had been granted title over the plot of his house, a deal brokered by the owner of the village's fishing fleet with the family that had owned all the land thereabouts.

Every night his great-grandfather would take a wax splint spluttering with dripping flame from the fire in the hearth, and would climb a ladder on the outside of the house to reach the big lamp which he had built on the flat, stone roof of the house, and he would illuminate the sky. Not only the village fishing fleet, returning at night or in fog with below decks stuffed with writhing bass, pilchard, cod, mullet, turbot; but also passing merchant ships and navy frigates would come to rely on the flickering yellow light alone on the cliff edge and would know to keep a distance and steer south east for another half an hour so that the reefs of the great bay would be missed and the headland could be cleared and the sanctuary of the village reached.

Sam had reached the house now, and he lay his bags

down on the concrete yard which is bordered at the front by the low whitewashed wall that he could see so clearly from the brow of the hill. The wall protected much of the area around the house from the south westerly breeze which most often blows across the bay. He scanned the view. The currents that had created such a ferment in the smaller bay of the village were strong out here too, and he could see the lines of the currents like threads spinning through the water, pale twisting lines one after the other in the green of the water and the waves cresting in white flashes all over the bay. The hot blue August sky was streaked towards the west with thin, wispy clouds that trailed off like fingers towards the horizon.

'Ah,' he said, nodding, 'that's what's doing it. That's brought the rip – rain coming tonight. Too much pressure before the rain gets out.'

He wasn't talking to himself; he was talking to his house.

'Devil's fingers, see?' he asked, pointing to the clouds' edges on the horizon. 'Only in August,' he explained, his rough hand brushing pebbles from the top of the wall. 'Be fine by the weekend.'

The knowledge of the rain to come reminded Sam that he would need to set about varnishing straight away if he was to allow time for it to dry by nightfall, so he turned back to the house, opened up the heavy wooden front door and then carried his bags into the low ceilinged kitchen.

The room was much as it had been when his mother collapsed on the floor over by the window ten years ago, felled by such a massive stroke that by the time the paramedic team had reached the village and then scrambled after the distraught giant of a man who was charging ahead of them back to the house, her heart had given up and she lay cold and dead on the stone floor. Sam's only real alteration had been to replace the iron cold store with a gas powered fridge four years ago. This was powered by bottled gas he collected every month from the delivery van which stopped at the top of the hill out of the village where the coast path starts.

Now he unpacked the few items he needed to buy regularly – milk, butter, cheese into the fridge, two bars of soap and some toilet paper for the toilet outside at the back of the house; a newspaper. He never needed much more than this. All his vegetables he grew himself in a big patch to the west side of the house, protected from the salty wind by a thick hedge, and his meat he bartered in great chunks from two of the local farmers in return for labour. He grew tomatoes and cucumbers outside in a glass and lead hothouse, which was the old warning light which his grandfather dismantled from the roof of the house when the local council built the new lighthouse on the headland in the 1920s.

He checked the thermostat setting of the fridge.

'We can turn you back up next week,' he said. 'End of August, weather will be turning, you won't need so much of our gas, you greedy bugger.'

He lay the newspaper down on the long wooden kitchen table, and walked through the arch into the dark dining room where his mother used to sleep on a cot in the corner. She moved out of the little side bedroom at the back of the house when she felt her only child was of the age to need his own room, and Sam still slept there. In his bedroom he changed into his work overalls, and then he went outside to set about varnishing the new cladding.

Isobel had showered already in the little hotel room. She padded naked around the room, her hair wrapped up in one of the white hotel towels, her skin still with drops of water on it.

The room was big enough to take a double bed in the centre, with a desk against one wall with a television and phone and kettle grouped together. She walked over to the glass doors and pulled aside the net curtains, and the blue green water of the village bay was right in front of her. She opened the doors, and immediately felt the sun once more on her body. There was a veranda for the room, with a table and chair on it, but she stayed in the doorway for the moment.

The hotel – long, low and white – was built in the 1920s into the eastern cliff of the village, so that the rooms looked back out over the bay and across to the beach. She could see the lifeboat which had landed and had been brought up onto the beach, and there were still crowds there. She looked away from it, up to the western headland on the other side of the bay. She remembered it all so well. The one road out of the village rose steeply up to the headland from beyond the far end of the shore, and at the top of the hill where the headland starts you could bear off onto a cliff path which would take you around the headland and over to the huge bay on the other side.

When she was about fifteen, about the time she was working in the bookshop on Saturdays, she would walk over to the big bay on her own to swim. She used to love the feeling of swimming alone in the water early on summer mornings before the crowds arrived, and the echoing silence over there, compared to the chatter of the village and its curved little beach.

She recalled now the last time she had been in the village. It was ten years ago, when she was twenty five. She had been home only three hours, and she and her mother had already come to blows, ending up staring angrily at each other in the little front room. She remembered it clearly, slamming the front door of the little cottage in the street two back from the beach and walking, furious, up to the hotel to sit in the bar and drink. She drank all evening, and almost went upstairs with a hopeful businessman who was staying in the hotel, but finally slipped away and stumbled back through the dark village streets.

Her mother found her in the morning, asleep outside the front door, curled up under the Victorian glass porch. They had breakfast together, and then she left, and never came back.

Well, she was here again now, and this time staying at the hotel. She had never stayed in a room here before. She stood up and looked at herself in the mirror on the wardrobe door, pulled off the towel from her head and worked her fingers through her thick, damp hair. She felt sorry now for the businessman, he must have had his hopes up. She remembered teasing him with her party trick: putting out lit matches between her forefinger and thumb, and staying quite still with the extinguished burnt match on her skin. Each time he tried to do it, he yelped and dropped the burning match.

'How do you do that?'

'The secret,' she said, 'is not to care that it hurts.' She didn't tell him she had seen Peter O'Toole do this in *Lawrence of Arabia*.

Isobel turned away from the mirror. For the last two days, ever since she had first heard, Isobel had imagined being here in the hotel, back in the village, with the sea and the silence and the great skies of her childhood.

She was here now. At last.

Sam had finished the varnishing now. He packed up the brush and the varnish pot in one of the aluminium sheds against the back wall of the house, and he looked back at the fresh cladding.

'That's a good coat,' he said encouragingly. 'Shrug off that easterly when it blows the rain down on you.'

He decided that he had enough time to go for a walk over the beach before his tea at six o'clock. He took the stone steps which led from a gap in the wall at the front of the house down about seventy or eighty feet to the top of the beach. The steps were laid by his grandfather and his father before the war, narrow concrete steps they had painstakingly made using wooden frames in which to set the concrete.

As he walked down, he looked out over the long, wide bay in front of him. The sun had shifted further over to the west and the clouds were banking darkly now above the far headland. The sea was a deep green, disturbed in its depths. He stepped patiently down each concrete ledge. He could see cormorants out on the surface of the water, ducking down occasionally and re-appearing further away after swimming black and wet through the water scavenging for sprats.

Once he was on the beach he walked over the rocks which were wrapped in bristling mussels. The sun created flashing mirrors from the pools of sea water left by the ebbing tide, and Sam looked about him both casually and specifically: greeting the flock of sea-finches and checking the depths of pools for evidence of crab and noting which people were on the beach today and glancing at the position of the sun over the far headland to see how much further west it was sitting now as August came to an end. He looked out for anything which might have been usefully left by the retiring tide.

As he left the rocks and walked down over the sand towards the edge of the water where the surf was noisy now, he passed a group of people standing and listening to one person reporting the death of the holidaymaker in the next door bay earlier in the day. One of the group called out:

'Sam! You heard about it?'

Sam recognised the short man with the round belly pushing out from an old grey T-shirt. He was often on the beach at low tide, and came over the headland from the village with a net to scour the rock pools of the great bay for prawn and crab. He was retired, and he talked a great deal. His face was animated now as he gave the group of holidaymakers his views on the tragedy earlier in the day.

'Yes, I heard,' said Sam carefully, and he continued walking towards the shore.

He did not wish to discuss it, because he knew that the only thing he had to say about the matter – that the man had died because he had not had the sense to learn about the ocean and its ways before allowing first his children and then himself into it – would not satisfy or please the people. If he stopped to be with this group, he would just be quiet, because he would have nothing more to add, and it would be the sort of quietness which was disturbing, and there would be a sourness in the air.

He walked on, and saw on the sand a fishing line that had been washed ashore. He bent to pick it up: a garish purple lure made of rubber with two rusty hooks, probably snagged on the rocks by one of the bass fishing boats that trawled steadily up and down the great bay when the waters ran quicker and the bass were feeding. He would keep it, grease the rusty hooks and use it himself on those occasional dark evenings when he rowed his own little boat up and down the bay.

'Nothing more then?' he asked the beach.

Over the years the tides had littered this huge, wide bay with such a range of things, a great store-house of man-made things from all over the world, natural things, animals. Sam now felt so attuned to the working rhythm of the beach that when a fat seal was caught struggling in the dip of the sand he could see how the warmer currents of that particular year might have confused the seal's sense of direction and led him astray from the deeper waters to get caught on this shore. When a half-broken packing case lay splintered in a rock pool he could almost see it slipping off the deck of a merchant ship two hundred miles away because an idle hand had failed to secure the lashings firmly during a high wind.

Things didn't arrive here by accident. The world

operated with quiet efficiency, and everything in it was linked together and was part of the world, and it was really only in the last ten years – when he had been living alone in the house and when he had stopped having to travel away to find paid work on building sites and he had found that he could live on what money he had or earned from occasional bartered labour – that Sam had become settled in his skin and felt such gentle happiness that sometimes he would stop what he was doing and would quietly sit wherever he was and let the salty tears trickle over his battered old face and into the lines of his smiling lips.

She didn't plan to leave the hotel room today. There would be enough time to do the things she had to do while she was here, there was no rush. And she had no desire to go straight back into the village with all the talk that there would be of the drowning.

It was late afternoon, and her eyes had just opened as she lay inside the white cotton sheets of the bed. It was delightful to know that she could lie here in the silence with the curtains shifting in the warm breeze and the sound of the surf outside. She could hear seagulls every so often, but no voices. She breathed quietly and gratefully.

Nobody knew she was here. She couldn't think of anyone who knew she was here. And she didn't have to tell her mother, who at this time of day would normally have been preparing a light supper for herself, the radio on in the kitchen, just a few hundred yards away, in the little house still in the street two back from the promenade.

In the front room where the television was and where her mother would probably have eaten, there might have been cards from Isobel on the mantlepiece. It was an unspoken agreement they came to, that they would keep each other informed occasionally about each other's existence. Isobel began it, sending a postcard a few months after the final argument, and a month later a postcard of the village arrived at her flat in the city. Isobel remembered the words: '*Dear Isobel, Autumn is upon us here in the village sooner than last year. The tourists now are all gone and the village is quiet. I have suffered a cold, but it is over now. The boiler in the kitchen has been replaced. Your loving mother.*'

The card sat on Isobel's breakfast table for days and she would look at it every time she sat down to eat. Finally, she put it face down on a bookshelf, and now it sat there with a pile of similar cards stacked on top of it. She wondered whether her mother did the same, but she suspected not: she guessed that her mother put her cards out on the mantlepiece. She could imagine her talking about them to neighbours who dropped in for coffee: 'Oh look Jean, another card from Isobel. We had such a lovely chat on the telephone last night, she is doing so well. I am so proud of her. Such a shame that she has so little time to get back here, she works too hard.'

Or maybe she didn't. Maybe Isobel was wrong, maybe her mother never mentioned her to her friends. She doubted it. That proud, stubborn, awkward woman – she wouldn't have let a mere neighbour know that she hadn't spoken to her daughter for ten years.

Tomorrow, once she had picked up the death certificate from the registrar in the village, she would have to go through her mother's things. She would have to go through everything in the little terraced house, on her own.

But not yet. Let's leave her now. Isobel was still tired, and she would spend the rest of the day quietly in her room, ordering some room service, sitting out on the veranda as the sun went down over the eastern headland.

She was calm, and later on, as she lay in the darkened room with the windows open to the sea, she lay asleep with a pretty, faint smile on her face.

When Sam went to bed that night, the rain that had threatened began to patter down gently on the roof of the house. There had been a deep flush of burnt orange over the western headland at dusk that indicated drier weather would follow soon.

'Might be some mist tonight though,' Sam had said to the kitchen as he looked through the window washing up the supper dishes. 'So hot earlier in the week, all that condensation, I reckon it'll bring the mist out at sea. Could have some rollers by the morning too.'

Outside in the dark the rain stopped not long after Sam had turned off the gas light in his bedroom. The warm currents of August air that swirled and flowed miles out at sea took shape here and there and gradually a damp spray of mist settled on the water far out from the shore and began to exert slow heavy pressure on the ocean. Bass and pollack and mackerel and jellyfish and eels and dogfish and even a school of dolphins four miles south west of the lighthouse began to feel the sea slowly churn in reaction to the weight of the mist, and long, low rolling waves began to flow back towards the shore where, as the tide reached its height just before midnight, they swelled up to their peak, hesitated in their full, tumultuous weight and then burst down on the shallow waters with a roar.

Sam slept uneasily. The growing volume of the surf invaded his dreams and his heavy body twitched to some unknown discord. There was a noisy mingling of shapes and faces and water in his dream, and it seemed like a voice calling louder and louder. At one point he sat up with a start and sweat on his forehead, saying aloud:

'What's this then? What's this?'

He sat still in the dark of his room, his eyes wide open and listening, but all he could hear were the waves. Still later in his dream the voice returned, but now joined by others, screaming it seemed, screaming with fear and panic and despair.

Two

The next morning Sam awoke to the sound of a cat calling from outside his bedroom window. He lay in bed for a few minutes while his eyes cleared and he prepared himself for the day. The room was narrow, with a single bed, a dark chest of drawers and a wardrobe, the stone walls covered with thin ply. When he was first given this room by his mother when he was twelve years old, the bare stone walls glistened with either dew or ice every morning, and in the winter when his mother would wake him by bringing in a cup of tea there would be clouds of steam wafting from the cup.

He wondered whether to walk over to Bridge's farm today, to continue rebuilding the wall of an old stone outhouse where the farmer wintered his cows. Occasional work like this earned him good returns – the farmer had promised him one of his pigs and a couple of lambs at slaughter time in the autumn, and Sam would butcher these himself and store all the joints in an old chest freezer which the farmer kept for him.

When he was a young man there was little or no work of this kind in the area, because each family had sons of its own who could build walls. Now the young men of the village and the surrounding farms left home when they could, seeking office work or anything that would pay a regular wage. Why would anyone stay, with so little hope of earning a living? The fishing catches had been savaged, the mines had closed, the farms automated. There was nothing now but the demands of the tourists who knew so little about the village; to them it was little more than a setting for their holidays, a picturesque backdrop.

But when he was young, and his mother told him he must stop his schooling and find work, it was a different matter. Occasionally, if he was lucky, he would walk for miles to a job on a building site, two pieces of greased bread and some fruit wrapped up in a cloth under his arm, returning home hours after the sun had dipped below the western headland of the great bay. But mostly there was nothing for him in the area, and so he began what led to two decades of an itinerant life, travelling with a gang of other men of his age from the village to the big cities hundreds of miles away, sometimes even to other countries, joining armies of other labourers to build the tower blocks and skyscrapers which swept across the country back then in the '60s and '70s.

Whenever he could he would return home, and with his mother they would sit at the kitchen table with the paraffin lamp and count his earnings and put little bits away here and there in savings accounts which she would set up for him in the village with a worried frown, looking over her shoulder for fear that someone in the queue would overhear and rob her of her son's savings.

And those times at home for Sam were so precious for him he filled every waking moment he could with the sea and the bay and the shoreline, sometimes in the summer sleeping down on the beach and waking himself up in the night so he could hear the rustle of crabs on the sand and the beautiful never-ending noise of the surf. Often he would lie awake on the sand with the stars spread across the sky and he would listen intently to the surf, cupping his hands around his ears to focus the sound, and he would know that the gentle crashing of the surf was created by thousands and millions of individual noises as pebbles were thrown against each other and each grain of sand rubbed against the other as the sea heaved and tugged from the depths. He would use all his strength to concentrate and try and separate out one individual noise from the whole symphony, because somehow he thought if he could know that he was listening to one precise sound within it all then he would at last be part of it himself. But he could never succeed, and at night as he lay awake hundreds of miles away in a cheap boarding house with five other men snoring and moaning in their sleep on flimsy narrow beds he would imagine he was on the beach and would try to think what one tiny individual component of the surf would sound like, and sometimes he would visualise that sound like a pure glow in the dark and would sleep once more.

The cat was still calling from the window.

'All right little one, you can come in,' Sam said, and he got out of bed and padded in blue nylon pyjamas to the window. He opened it, and a black cat sprang past him onto the floor, where it stood arching its back with relief. There were several feral cats that lived on the cliffs, but only this one had decided to establish a relationship with the big man. If it was too tired for hunting field mice or stalking bird nests for vulnerable young, it would appear at the house and Sam would offer to share one of his meals.

The cat hated the rain, and Sam knew that it would not have enjoyed last night's weather.

'I could have told you yesterday it would be wet last night, you should have come in before, saved yourself a soaking.' The cat watched Sam dress, then nudged against his calf, wiping his fur on Sam's trousers. 'All right cat, enough of that, breakfast is coming.'

Sam walked out through the dark main room with its heavy oak sideboards and ceiling-high cupboards and into the kitchen. He stood at the sink where the dishes from his supper the previous evening were clean and dry on the draining board, and he poured himself a glass of water and looked out through the window at the bright morning. Out at sea, at the point on the left where the horizon was cut off by the headland, a Navy frigate was steaming due west. A scattering of seagulls were swooping and hovering over one area of the bay, and Sam picked up the binoculars from the window ledge, and then could see the shadow in the water where the gulls were gathering.

'Mackerel,' he said. 'Shoal of mackerel, probably, too small for bass.'

Last night's turbulent weather had cleared, and he felt relief, as though a storm had passed him by. He said to the kitchen:

'Didn't sleep well. Don't think I'll go to Bridge's. Stay at the bay today, enjoy the day.'

Does it matter that Sam talks to his kitchen, his house? Well, he could never have pinpointed the moment at which it happened, and perhaps there was no moment. Over the years away on the building sites when he learned his trade, he learned too about his fellow man and he learned to look at an angle always so that he could go quietly about his work and not attract attention. For although most men were wary of his size and his huge arms and muscled neck which could carry double the weight of bricks on his massive shoulders than any other man, still they would goad the great giant when they felt brave in a pack and would stare at him with sneering ugly faces. Sam would launch himself furiously at his tormentors and it would take five of them eventually to kick him to the floor and he would cover his face with his hands as they kicked him until their own exhaustion made them stop.

Perhaps the change in Sam was a slow movement like the way the cloud's shadow could slowly darken the whole cliff of the great bay, the line of the shadow on the ground racing over fields and hedges and gorse until the whole four miles of the bay's cliffs were in shade. Perhaps it was like that. Because now he did not distinguish between what he saw as the living components of the world: people, animals, the sea, his house, the farmer's tractor, the food he put in his mouth. He saw the worth or value of each, and he admired the contribution which anything could make to the functioning of the world, and he learned to turn his glance from the destructive, the useless, anything which he could not place within the world as he understood it.

He began to prepare porridge. The cat watched him while he stirred the oats in the pan, and once it was ready he poured porridge into one of the thick china bowls, wide and creamy-coloured which his mother had bought after her wedding, and a much smaller amount into a saucer. He set them both down on the long kitchen table and he and the cat ate breakfast, the cat's tail brushing the table top with pleasure.

It was still early morning, and the sun was not yet high enough in the sky to be visible from Sam's house, but in the village on the other side of the headland the empty streets shimmered with the hot August morning light.

The long white hotel overlooking the village shone brilliantly under the cloudless blue sky, and the silent early morning smelt of salt and dust and the first hint of the bakery two streets back from the promenade. Then the whine of the milk float's electric motor, clanking bottles and someone's footsteps echoing down another street.

A heavy sea mist hung over the water on the horizon between the two points of the village's bay, and the surface of the water as it approached the village was rippled with waves that slapped against the rocks exposed by the low tide.

Poor Isobel. She's not lying asleep in her room any more. With that sweet little smile. She's not even out on her veranda, sitting in a long white hotel cotton dressing gown, sipping coffee and looking at the rocks of the beach in the fresh summer morning air. It would have been a nice, gentle start to her long day.

No, when she woke an hour ago, while it was still dark, she lay awake with feelings so familiar to her: the dawn sensation of being a bad person, of being wrong. Once, she had talked at length with a man who was recovering from a heart operation on the ward, and she could never forget how he told her that each day he woke with a sense of thrilled anticipation, of wonder at what he might achieve that day. He had felt this every morning of his life, even in the early years of his childhood. Isobel had wondered about this man for a long time. For Isobel, each new day appeared as a challenge at best; at worst

34

– and lately this seemed more usual – as an unwelcome surprise.

So no, she hadn't leaped out of bed with a song in her heart. That's not her way. She had lain in bed for a while, fruitlessly anxious, and then for want of anything more constructive she had dressed and gone straight to her mother's house. In an old track suit and trainers, she had left the hotel and walked down the hill into the village. They were her footsteps we heard.

She's sitting on the stone floor of the glass porch of her mother's house. She has the keys in her pocket, but now she's here, she can't go in. She is talking.

'It's easy for you to say that.' Her words, soft and lonely inside the closed glass doors of this little Victorian porch. 'But I keep trying, I keep trying to do what you say. You make it sound as though it should be so easy. Why do you make it sound so easy?'

Do you know the story of Abelard and Héloise? It's a sort of love story, or has become so in the retellings over the centuries. The story is true: they existed.

It's twelfth century France, and the most exciting, the most vigorous young theologian of Paris, Abelard, falls in love with his young pupil, Héloise. They have a child, born in shameful secret. Abelard is castrated by his lover's angry uncle. Héloise is banished to a nunnery, where she spends the decades of the rest of her life. Abelard lives to become a prominent church leader. They never meet again, but they write to each other, she seeking solace for her loneliness in this world without him, he pouring out his longing while at the same time counselling her to remain strong. They are buried side by side many years later, never together again in life. Their letters, drenched in erotic longing, are extraordinary. You should read them.

This is important about Isobel: she did read them. She read them when she was fifteen, in the bookshop about a hundred yards away on the seafront. While the old owner dozed in his chair at the back, and the sun tried to make its way through the book-filled windows, Isobel sat beside the till and read the letters between Abelard and Héloise.

And when the old man woke one afternoon and found what she was reading, and he was able to quote to her many of the letters from memory, she was not embarrassed. He was not trying to impress her. He recited: '*So intense were the fires of lust which bound me to you that I set those wretched, obscene pleasures, which we blush even to name, above God as above myself.*' And then he himself blushed, and retired again to the back room, and she continued to read, pretending that she couldn't hear him crying.

But she knew, even then, what the letters were about. She knew, without knowing the details, that they represented some soaring tragedy in the life of this plain, tired old man. She knew that they also spoke to her as though the protagonists were in front of her, eight hundred years on, telling her their story. She understood completely then, aged fifteen, that she would never meet a man as complete as Abelard, and she felt light-headed with the knowledge.

So here she is now, in the porch, still talking to him after all these years. Isobel is reciting now too:

'*Remember, I implore you, what I have done, and think how much you owe me. Now the end is proof of the beginning. In the name of that God to whom you have dedicated yourself, I beg you to restore your presence to me in the way you can – by writing me some work of comfort, so that in this at least I may find increased strength. I beg you, think what you owe me…*'

Sam cleared the last concrete step from his house to the beach, and set off west along the wide shoreline which was left by the ebbed tide. The cold air and the clear early morning sky refreshed him, and he walked in his rubber soled plimsolls along the wet sand. He thought he would walk half way along the great bay, about two miles, and check to see that the night's waves had not damaged the collection of rowing boats, one of them his, which were tied up at the foot of the cliff there.

At this hour he was alone on the beach, and he took in the whole scene which every day was created anew by the tide and the wind and the birds and living fabric of the beach.

His mind was occupied still with the uncertainties of the night. Sam did not like the feeling of doubt which nights like this gave him.

Recently he had been suffering from these bad dreams, and it felt to him that his mind at night was often busy with thoughts of his father, although he could never recall the content of the dreams he must have been having. He had been puzzling over the cause of these disturbances, as they did not seem to come from anywhere that he could recognise, and they did not seem to lead any-where. It was an imprecise, uncertain awareness of his father that he felt during these moments, and it seemed as though he were examining one of his tools which was not working properly but could not establish the cause even though he carefully explored each moving part and gently applied pressure with his thumb and forefinger all over the mechanism.

He was four years old when his father was lost at sea, hurled with gigantic force from the prow of the village lifeboat by a towering wave half a mile out to sea from the headland. It was the middle of the night and the crew were struggling to reach a fishing vessel whose engine had failed returning back to harbour just as the weather fell into a storm. The vessel's plight had been reported by the lighthouseman who had seen the SOS flashes from the ship's main lantern, and Sam's father had been the first of the lifeboat crew to be woken when the lighthouseman hammered on the door of the house on his way to the village. In the wind and the rain and the night his father had run after him, and once in the village they ran shouting through the empty streets. Within ten minutes the eight-man crew was wading through the surf on the beach, pushing the lifeboat beyond the breakers until they were all aboard, six of them rowing, one on the tiller at the stern and his father on the prow, shouting instructions ('Pull, lads, pull... heavy on starboard now, I see the ship, I see her...'), the huge waves crashing over his head and soaking the men as the boat reared up ten, eleven, twelve feet to the peak of the wave; and then stopped and was almost motionless and weightless for a second until with a sickening rush it smashed back down into the trough and the men dug their oars into the water again and took two, three strokes as the boat climbed the next wave. When they were about fifty yards from the ship and they could hear the fishermen calling out, fearful as they were pulled closer and closer to the headland reefs, the lifeboat was surprised by an enormous wave which followed seconds after another and hit the prow so hard that Sam's father's powerful fingers slipped from the running strake and he was thrown overboard and immediately plunged down into the black, freezing turmoil of the waves, surfacing once or twice with a blurred image of the house and his wife and his little son before he was sucked down again with a rush to about twenty feet and his body filled with the ice water and he was lost.

Sam remembered the day when his mother wailed for

hours alone on the beach and women from the village kept him from leaving the house to go to her. After that day, his mother never spoke to him of his father's death, and he never saw her cry again.

Sam climbed up over one of the large outcrops of rock that stretched down almost as far as the low tide's edge, and clumsily hopped from one rock to another, steadying himself with his hand here and there, and pausing to examine each pool of water and some deep crevices where he knew tasty crabs the size of his bare hands were waiting out the time before the tide would bring the sea water back to cover them.

'You just stay there my friends,' he said. 'I'm coming with my bucket tomorrow. One or two of you is going home to meet my cooker.'

And he laughed, and with the breath that cleaned through him as he stood on one of the rocks looking out at the bay as the first signs of the sun began to appear golden over the headland to the left, he felt the unaccountable anxieties of the night flow away from him and he was refreshed.

He clambered down again and returned to the sand and continued his walk towards the centre of the bay, the water lapping just a few feet to his left and his plimsolls sinking into the wet sand a little each time he took a step. Behind him the sun was swiftly clearing the headland, and even at this early hour he could feel the heat of the rays on the back of his shirt and on his hair, and ahead of him the whole bay was precise and bright and absolutely clear and filled with light.

Then he noticed a dark shape lying forty or fifty feet ahead of him in the shallows.

'Hello,' he said. 'What's this? Seal again? Seal gone and got himself lost again?'

As he approached the shape he could see no movement, and then he was closer still, and soon he was standing right over it, his great body casting a shadow over what he could see now was a human being.

'What's this then? Not a seal this time.'

He bent down and put his hands on the wet clothes and gently pulled the shoulder so that the body rolled onto its back and he could see that the body was that of a little girl. He put his hand against her forehead, then pressed his first finger into a vein on her neck, brushing her dark hair off her face with his other hand. Her skin was white, absolutely white, and her eyes were closed.

'Now what are you doing here?' he asked. He frowned. This was an arrival on the beach for which it was difficult to account. 'But I think you may have some life in you.'

He scooped his arms under her soaking clothes and lifted her up out of the shallow water and walked back up the beach twenty yards or so and lay her down again on the dry sand. He put his right hand over his left and pushed both down onto the girl's chest, repeated this four or five times with sharp thrusts, then turned the body onto its side. He did this once more, then again, and all the time he remembered seeing the lifeguards perform this action on the village beach when he was a young man and a surfer had been dragged unconscious from the waves.

'Can't do anything else for you,' he said, repeating the operation once more, 'this is all I know.'

On the fourth turn of her body, the little limbs shook, and her mouth opened and a trickle of seawater flowed from her mouth into the sand.

He laughed. 'There, you see, I told you!'

Once more he pumped her chest, and this time when he rolled her to the side a gush of water choked from her mouth and her eyes flickered. He lifted her up again and held her in his arms and patted her back with solid thumps, and more water was spat out from her mouth and her legs wriggled.

'All right then,' he said, and put the little body back on the sand.

He knelt down again and pulled her back up off the floor, holding her shoulders so that she was sitting with her legs stretched out, and at that moment the girl opened her eyes wide and stared straight at him with her hair and one side of her face covered in sand, and she smiled.

Three

Sam smiled back. 'Well now, what do you say? What have we here then? What's this on the beach now then?'

The girl continued to look up at him and held his gaze, smiling still. She did not say anything.

Sam looked at her little frame, drenched in sea water. 'What are you – five, six years old? No more, I don't think. Well now that's something. We'd better get you warmed up.'

He leant forward further to pick the child up, but she tucked her legs in, leant back on her hands and stood up. Then she put out her right hand and grabbed Sam's hand and tugged, until he, laughing now, stood up too. She turned to face the sun, tugged at him once more, and the two of them began to walk back the way Sam had come, towards his house.

Sam was laughing out loud now, and his big chuckles rang out across the empty sun-filled beach.

'So you're in charge now, is it? I find a half-drowned little girl lying face down in the water, and the next minute she's wearing the trousers?'

He couldn't stop his laughter. The girl looked up at

him quizzically at first, still holding his hand, and then once more she smiled such a soft smile, and then turned to face the sun again.

They walked together back along the beach, Sam chuckling every now and then, saying, 'Even that seal we had here last year, he took a couple of hours to get himself sorted, but not this one!'

The sun was shining strongly straight at them, and when he glanced down at the little girl, Sam was surprised again, because now her clothes appeared to be completely dry. He could see that she was wearing a black dress, pulled in at the waist, with a pattern of white bows over it, an old fashioned child's dress which went down just below her knees. Her feet were bare, and hardly imprinted themselves on the wet sand, compared to the heavy gouges that Sam's shoes made beside her. She had straight dark black hair to her shoulders, and this too was dry now, the ends playing in the light shore breeze.

As they passed the outcrop of rock that Sam had stood upon earlier, the girl let go of his hand and ran over to the rock, carefully climbed up the first two or three boulders avoiding the sharp mussels, and then peered into one of the deep cracks within, where damp seaweed and glistening anemones hung all over and trickles of sea water covered the barnacles. She looked back at Sam, who was still walking towards her, and she grinned excitedly and pointed towards the dark underbelly of the rock. He climbed up beside her and glimpsed some movement in the salty shadows.

'Crab?' he asked her. 'You see a crab?'

This time it was her turn to laugh, a light tinkling sound that hovered like glitter in the bright empty morning air. She leapt from the rock down to the sand, and ran about in circles, her dark eyes wide with happiness. Sam crouched on the rock still and watched her, as her black cotton dress flowed in the breeze and she stretched her hands out wide from her sides.

'Well, this I don't understand,' he said to the rocks.

He did not particularly distinguish children from adults in his life, as for him they often appeared together as a whole, a human-ness which so often glanced across his own perception of the world. He had no cause to play with children, and he viewed them as though he himself were still a child: they were part of the whole human society around him, different ages, different sensibilities, but all of the human kind.

When he was little, he would ask his mother sometimes, as he lay in the cold little room and looked up at her as she sat beside his bed stroking his hair, why two boys from his class had thrown stones at a dog; or why on another occasion a gang of them had broken into an empty house, smashing the thick door which had curved mouldings on the front which had been turned by carpenters years before; or why he had ended up in a fight which had begun when a little girl had shouted names at him which made no sense about his house and his mother and others had joined in and he had rushed at them, scattering them as some shrieked and some laughed and he flailed about with his hard little fists and tears in his eyes. His mother would smile, say 'Shhh,' and he would drift to sleep with the heart shape of her face imprinted in his mind.

'But where has she come from?' Sam asked the rocks. 'Child doesn't suddenly appear on the beach. Where's the boat that's sunk, where's the family looking for her?'

The girl was still playing on the sand that was beginning to absorb the heat from the early morning sun, and instead of just running now she was turning and spinning, and Sam realised that she was dancing, her arms now reaching up high to a point, then sweeping low as she curved and bobbed to some tune that perhaps she could hear, but on the beach all the sound was of the surf and the seagulls overhead.

'Well, she must be somebody's,' Sam said, 'better find out whose. Get some breakfast, then I'll take her to the village, find out.'

He clambered down the rocks and walked towards her. She saw him, and ran towards him, breathing fast from her activity, the still white of her face flecked with red and her mouth wide with silent laughter. She came straight up to him, and took both his huge heavy hands in hers, and swayed her arms and her body, looking up at him and smiling and nodding.

Sam realised that she wanted him to dance too. He began to chuckle again, then his deep laugh could be heard again across the beach as he hopped clumsily from one heavy foot to the other, and the slight, dark little girl in her flowing black dress and the tall, broad man with his thick sandy hair danced a whirling, circling dance on the beach, the little girl's back arching out as she pulled against his grip and both of them laughing as they spun round and round and round and round.

After sitting in the porch of her mother's house, Isobel had gone back to bed. Now, later in the morning she sat at one of the tables in front of the hotel, eating a late breakfast. She had the local newspaper propped up in front of her, and she was reading about the death in the village bay yesterday afternoon. As she spooned scrambled egg into her mouth, she read about the victim and the family he had left behind.

The man was a tourist, had been on holiday with his wife and children. The sheer randomness of his death, its lack of any sense, interested Isobel. All the actions the man must have taken yesterday, from waking up to dying, they all led meaninglessly to an absurd conclusion. What tiny action or incident could have occurred differently during his last day, so that he didn't end up choking on sea water?

She could imagine Abelard setting this as one of his

metaphysical debates at the pulpit in Paris. In fact one of his most famous debates was titled *Sic et Non: Yes and No*. The debate presented a range of conflicting evidence covering 158 different theological issues, and he invited his listeners – mostly young theological students – to consider the different possible conclusions to each. Eight hundred years later, and Isobel is still a *Yes and No* person: an ambivalence about life which she knew alienated people.

Why was it that she could never feel these certainties which seemed to come to other people so freely? Her mother always used to chastise her for it, the way she would always see both sides of a case. 'Just for once, child, can't you see what's right, what's wrong? Why can't you?'

It made her hesitant still as an adult, doubtful of expressing views when she knew that she had no real feeling for them either way. It wasn't that she *felt* any the less; in fact, Isobel was if anything *too* kind, *too* compassionate. Her life in the city was filled with people who depended on her, people who found it difficult to cope, people who found it easier to cope by unburdening themselves on her. She instinctively was drawn to them, felt obliged to support them. It was, probably, why she ended up working in the hospital.

You see, Isobel is a good person. There is no doubt about that. No matter what her mother said; no matter what the Ward Sisters at the hospital say about her attitude. It doesn't matter that people find her unorthodox, difficult to comprehend.

It is important that we know this, about her: that she is good.

Randomness: it informed her life. The way she first left this village was random. She was still only half way through her A-level course at the local school when for no particular reason she took off with a boy she had been seeing at nighttime down by the lighthouse on the headland. She liked the way he lisped slightly when he said *th*, and she liked the way he talked about getting enough money to buy a boat and to sail away from the village forever. It never really concerned her that he might be what her mother called a *ne'er-do-well*, and when one night he said he was leaving for good the following day, that he had to go because some people were after him, she just said she would go too.

They found a room in a house in the city that belonged to some friends of his. Later she realised it was a squat. That was after he had left. But by then she was used to it, and the people in the house didn't find her strange, so she stayed on. Almost twenty years later, she still lived in the same house. Over the years it had been smartened up, turned into council housing, and she now had a self-contained flat in it, but some of the original people still lived nearby.

Everything was random.

Isobel ate breakfast in the sun, thinking about the man

drowning, about her mother, about nothing.

When Sam and the child got back to the house from the beach a sense of normality and routine seemed to return after the wonder of the early morning. Sam prepared porridge for the girl and as he explained to the kitchen what had happened she sat silently at the long table.

'Lying there face down in the water, no life in her it seemed, and then she's up and walking down the beach pretty as you please, and I look at her again, and blow me, she's dry already, her clothes and hair, completely dry. And then she has me dancing, old Sam, dancing on the beach!'

And he chuckled again as he ladled porridge out into a bowl, and then some too for him. He placed the bowls on the table and sat down beside the girl. The girl finished her food quickly.

'You hungry then?' Sam asked. 'How long were you out there in the water? How did you get there then?'

She looked at him, smiling once more, and then widened her eyes as though in a question and pushed her empty plate.

'You want some more? You'll have to have some bread and jam, porridge finished.' He got up and cut her two pieces of bread from a loaf and covered them with butter and jam, butter from the village grocery and jam that he had made last winter from the berries amongst the heather on the headland. She ate them quickly, then wiped her mouth on the sleeve of her black dress and grinned at him.

'You don't talk maybe,' said Sam after a while. 'That's all right. I talk all the time, but the house here, he doesn't talk. Some talk anyway, it doesn't mean anything. Cat doesn't talk. Talk's not so special. What's talk anyway? Talk doesn't make the porridge, talk doesn't fix the wall at the back of the house.'

The loud calls of seagulls broke the air from outside through the open front door.

'Seagulls,' said Sam. 'Buggers know we've had breakfast, hanging around for scraps. They can have the last bit of my porridge. I had some earlier.'

But before he could move the little girl took his plate and carried it outside and walked over the white concrete yard to the low wall that faced the sea. She spooned the last lumps of Sam's porridge out on to the flat part of the wall and as she tapped the spoon on the stone to shake off the last of the porridge one of the seagulls swooped down, its beating wings almost touching the girl's face. It snatched a piece of porridge in its beak, then was joined by two or three more with a great rushing of wings and excited callings until the porridge was gone, and all the time the girl jumped up and down on the concrete yard and clapped her hands and laughed delightedly. Sam watched from the doorway of the house and shook his head.

'Seagulls,' he called out to her. 'Eat anything they will.'

He looked at the girl as she leaped up and down in excitement. What should he do? She seemed healthy, so he wasn't worried about that. But she must belong to someone. There was no sign of any activity out in the big bay, no lifeboats searching for survivors of a stricken ship, no helicopters overhead. And the beach had been deserted.

Perhaps he would walk into the village with her and she might recognise someone or she would be recognised. He felt uncomfortable about this, about deliberately engaging in contact with others, but he would have to try. Perhaps everything would be done quietly.

Once the seagulls had departed, the girl walked back to the front door of the house, and for the first time her little face looked tired.

'You'd better lie down little one,' said Sam. 'You can lie down on mother's cot, have a sleep before we walk to the village.'

He led the girl into the gloomy front room and showed her the narrow bed that his mother had always used when the two of them were together in the house. It was pushed up against one corner, and at the foot was a heavy old chest of drawers.

'You have a rest on there, Sam will have a look through his old clothes, find you some shoes for our walk.'

As the girl lay on the cot and closed her eyes, Sam

opened the drawers of the chest and looked through the musty smelling collection of old clothes. He knew that his mother had always kept all his old clothes, and he had never bothered to clear these cupboards out after her death. Amongst the grey thin vests and shorts and socks, he found a pair of child's brown sandals, the leather straps frayed and the buckle on the left one loose but tied to the sandal with a piece of string. It must have been fifty years since he had last worn them.

While the child slept he sat in the old armchair with a needle and thread and carefully sewed the buckle back onto the shoe. When he was finished, he lay the sandals on the floor beside the cot, and he crept out of the room and through the kitchen back out into the yard.

Sam spent the next hour in the garden over on the other side of the yard, pulling up a few more potatoes, a couple of cabbages, carrots, turnip and tidying up the weeds. As he was pulling up the last stems, he sensed a presence, and looked up to see the girl at the end of the vegetable patch, gathering the discarded weeds into a neat pile. She was wearing Sam's old brown sandals. He came back over to her.

'You helping old Sam?' he asked gently. She continued to sweep the weed cuttings together, and when she was finished she looked up at him. He ruffled her black hair.

'Come on, we'd better go to the village.'

Four

Isobel's mind was filled with thoughts of the poor man's final day. She had begun to imagine it almost like a film, his life slipping away frame by frame as each action led slowly to the moment when he would enter the water. She decided after breakfast to walk up to the headland so she could get a different perspective on the village, to shake off these conundrums. She knew too that she was still avoiding the main reason for her visit, but what did it matter? It was too late now anyway. She packed a swimming costume, thinking she might be tempted to swim over on the big beach like she used to twenty years ago.

She walked down from the hotel to the promenade, which was busy now with holidaymakers, past her old shop, continued on to the end and then up the steep hill which she could remember now so clearly from nights out with the village boys. At the top was a sign leading the way to the coast path down towards the lighthouse which the boys leerily used to call Lovers Lane. It was there she had spent her last night in the village before leaving with her ne'er-do-well.

Just beside the sign was a wooden seat with an inscription on it, and Isobel sat down and placed her bag beside her and rested for a moment looking down over the village and the bay. The village of course looked small from up here, even smaller than it had felt when she first arrived yesterday. She watched the sun glint off the water and felt the heat of it now on her face.

She remembered the first time she made love when she was sixteen, down at the end of the path beside the lighthouse. She had no memory now of how she had felt about it – pleased, she would imagine, pleased that she had done it – but the idea of it still thrilled her. She found it exciting to think about making love to someone. These days, in the city, she still loved the anticipation that led up to sleeping with someone, and more than anything she loved to picture the man, his face, as he looked down on her, the intensity of his expression. She would project a previous lover's face onto someone she hoped to sleep with – always looking forward, always hoping that she would be taken by surprise, that the experience would carry her away. But usually it didn't. Usually her awareness of everything overwhelmed any spontaneity, and she made love with whoever it was out of kindness rather than passion. She thought she owed it to them.

The only thing that would concern her was how she imagined her mother would view it. Sometimes she could feel the older woman's disapproval chilling her from hundreds of miles away. She imagined her mother bitterly upbraiding her for not 'settling down', accusing her of being a 'tramp', warning her of the consequences that would inevitably result.

'You think life's exciting, you think it's about enjoyment. You think it's about just doing whatever you want. It's not. It's about duty, it's about responsibility. Your father would have told you that.'

'No he wouldn't. No, he wouldn't have said anything like that to me. He never said anything like that to me!'

This sort of conversation they played out so many times before she walked out ten years ago, and the echoes of it remained with her, like voices caught inside a bottle, to be released every now and then when she was alone. On these occasions she would give in to one of her curious, irrational weaknesses – popular psychology books, with titles like *Who Am I Now?* and *It's Time For Me*. She used to buy these anonymously over the internet, and if one of these moods gripped her she would read one in an evening, guzzling it down with a bottle of cheap wine alone in her flat. Afterwards, the book would be thrown into the bin, and it would sit in the dark amongst the empty supermarket meal packets, a hoisin sauce oozing over its pages, like discarded pornography.

Sitting high up here on the bench, with the sun strong overhead and the sea spread out before her, Isobel felt calm. She closed her eyes.

She had spoken about her mother last week to a kind, older doctor who worked in the hospital where she had been employed for the last five years as an orderly. They had sat together in the middle of the night in the staff room, after he had finished signing the time of death sheet for a young man who had been brought into A and E after a car accident.

'I am so tired of this,' he had said.

'Why do you do it?' she had asked him. 'You could leave.' Alternatives always presented themselves to Isobel. He had looked up at her, his eyelids sagging from exhaustion.

'If not me, then someone else has to do it. It's what I do, Isobel.' He had said this gently, not critically. Then he had asked her about her life. What was she doing here, an orderly on low pay, cleaning up bedpans in the night?

'You are young, you are beautiful. Why do you spend your life here? Me, I have no choice, I must do it now. I have responsibilities. You, you should make a change, it's not too late. Get away from all this.'

She told him how she had first left the village such a long time ago. She told him about the odd jobs she had taken over the years: working in shops, in an old people's home; sometimes just on the dole, sitting in parks and reading. She told him about the people she knew, about how she gave a bit of money to one or two of them she thought needed help. The boy in the flat below her who she shopped for, because he didn't like to go out. The sculptor she modelled for, who sometimes made love with her if his wife was out. She even told him about

Abelard and Héloise, about how one day she meant to write her own book, a book about love, certainty, longing, regret, survival.

She told the old doctor about her mother, their fights, the postcards she had been sending for the last ten years.

'She is alive. Don't you see? Your mother, she is alive. You shouldn't waste it. I think you like to pretend that she is dead.' He shook his head. 'There'll be lots of time for that when it is real, you know that. Don't wish it earlier. You should go and see her.'

Three days later she got the telephone call telling her that her mother had died.

Isobel opened her eyes again, and saw to her right a huge man walking towards her with a little girl at his side, walking hand in hand on the path towards the point at which it met the road by her seat. The man was strong, and his face and bare arms were brown and tough-looking. He was looking to his right away from her down to the village and the bay. Isobel suddenly recognised him from the curious comments yesterday in front of the drowning.

As they walked past her, Isobel looked at the little girl, probably his grand-daughter she thought, dressed in a curiously formal black dress. The girl stared silently straight back at Isobel and turned her little head to continue looking at her as they reached the end of the path and took the road away from the headland and back down into the village. Isobel continued to look into the girl's solemn dark eyes until she and the man disappeared from view down the slope of the hill.

Once Sam and the girl had reached the top of the headland on the steep narrow cut-through and began to descend again to the coast path on the other side, Sam thought he would show the girl the peregrine falcon who lived up here in the heights of the cliffs that overlooked the village. She had liked the seagulls, she would like to see the falcon. But as they approached the wooden bench at the top of the path he could see someone already sitting there, a good-looking woman with long, heavy hair. He took the little girl's hand firmly in his and did not stop and looked down over the bay as he walked past the woman and onto the road that led down into the village.

Sam was not sure what his plan was. He did not want a lot of fuss, and somehow thought that either the girl would recognise her parents or they her – she must be on holiday, and surely they would be looking for her? But still it made no sense, and he knew also that it was strange that he had found her so early in the morning when the beach was deserted.

'We'll just see,' he said, still gripping her hand as they neared the foot of the steep hill and reached the first houses at the end of the village. 'We'll go quietly, you tell me when we see your mum, and that'll be that. No fuss then.'

The girl looked up at him with a small frown as though she did not understand him.

Hand in hand they walked slowly along the promenade. It was late morning now and the sun was high over the village beach which was busy and noisy with holidaymakers. A family in swimming costumes walked across the road in front of them carrying ice creams from one of the cafés on the front, and stepped back onto the beach down the stone steps from the promenade where there was a gap in the railings. The breeze brought conflicting sounds of pop music from radios on the beach. Out in the surf there was a mixture of children and parents playing and a group of teenagers in wetsuits with surfboards. Sam paused by one of the benches and indicated to the girl that she should sit.

'You stay here for one minute, I'm going to buy the newspaper, see if they mention you.'

He pointed at the newsagent on the other side of the road, and she nodded back at him gravely. There might be something if she went missing yesterday, he thought.

He came back to the bench and sat beside her. As he leafed through the pages the girl sat very still. She did not seem to be interested in the families spread all over the beach, and in fact she showed no signs of recognising anything. She looked down at her feet and swung them back and forth, staring at the old brown sandals which

Sam had given her.

'Nothing in here about you,' Sam said.

The girl looked up from her shoes and smiled.

'Don't know what else to do really.'

He had thought that a missing little girl would have been the talk of the village, on top of all that business with the man drowning yesterday, and he had thought that he would overhear a conversation about it and somehow a reconciliation would have occurred. But he knew he couldn't go about himself asking if anyone knew the little dark eyed girl at his side – it was too long now since, too long a time away from people. He could not do that.

'What shall I do then?' he asked the bench.

It was an unsatisfactory piece of furniture, the wooden slats allowed to rot here and there from lack of regular coatings of paint and varnish against the sun and the waves which at the spring high tides would beat upon it. He crumbled a splintery edge between his rough fingers.

'No answers then?'

At this the girl jumped down off the bench onto the pavement and tugged at Sam's hand. She glared at him with wide eyes, and pulled at his arm.

'You want to go now? Where? You want to go some-where?'

She tried to pull him from the bench, her tiny body having no impact upon his great bulk, but she strained as though trying to go back the way they had come.

He laughed. 'She's not strong enough to shift me off you,' he told the bench, 'but she'll try though.'

Now the girl seemed more agitated, then she looked down again as a short man with a fat belly came up to them, Sam still laughing as the girl tugged at his arm.

'What's this Sam, got a new friend?'

Sam recognised the voice of the man who came prawn and crab fishing over on the big beach. He stopped laughing, stood up without looking at the man who was in front of them now eyeing them curiously.

'Didn't know you had relatives Sam.'

Sam looked past the man out to the strip of the horizon between the two curved headlands of the bay.

'No,' he said quietly, and then the girl tugged at his arm once more and they walked off back down the promenade.

As the two of them walked to the end of the prom-enade and then out onto the hill road out of the village, the man was still watching them from beside the bench. He continued to watch them for a couple of minutes, then he turned and crossed the street over to one of the cafés.

Isobel spent several hours on the beach of the great bay, anonymous on her towel on the sand amongst the holidaymakers who were spread out more widely on this huge bay than they were on the enclosed beach of the village. She lay in her swimming costume dozing under the hot August sun, and felt the pressure of the heat on her skin which glistened with suntan lotion. She breathed slowly and deeply with an image of the burning sun through her closed eyelids. The shouts of children who were building sandcastles and the noise of the surf and the conversations of people walking by slowly on the sand were all mixed together but softened by the breeze.

The beach was resting her and she was not thinking specifically now. After a while she got up and walked down to the water. The tide was on the way out again, and she walked in to her waist then fell forwards and swam through the low breaking waves, closing her eyes and ducking her head down into each wave so that the water covered her head and she could feel it all around her with a great explosion of sound. The water was cold but she had never been afraid of the cold water when she was a little girl and she began to duck dive down below the surface, opening her eyes in the salt water and feeling with her hands on the sandy floor for shells, then coming back up and breaking into the sudden sunlight and gasping out air.

She swam some more, then flipped onto her back and floated under the sun, waving her hands gently underwater to keep afloat. Squinting through the sharp light she could see the low curve of the cliffs all the way from

PATIENCE SWIFT

the headland on the right where the lighthouse stood
to the long stretch of clifftop which hung over the three
or four miles of the bay over to the other headland way
away over on the left. The cliffs were green and purple
with summer vegetation. Over on the right hand side of
the bay, tucked into the cliff itself, was a white cottage,
tiny in the distance with a line of steps going down to
the beach. Isobel remembered this had long ago been
the lighthouse, before she was born, and where an old
woman had lived when she was at school who used to
come and clean for her mother, polishing the brass step
early in the morning every week.

The woman had once invited Isobel to tea at her
cottage – an invitation made shyly, which Isobel even
then had perceived as a charged request, expressing
some need on the woman's part which Isobel felt she
should satisfy. She probably thought she should extend
the invitation to her employer's daughter; but Isobel also
felt that she wanted to tell her something. Of course
she had accepted, and in fact visited the woman several
times. She encouraged her to tell her tales of the village
from her youth, and once she attempted to repay her by
bringing a present of a book from the bookshop, but the
old woman was horrified and refused it; it was because
she thought she would have to find a present to give in
return. Isobel never found out what it was that was on
the woman's mind, and at some point she just stopped
going.

She closed her eyes and stretched her neck so her head lay back in the water and she could feel the heat of the sun all over her.

'How fertile with delight is your body, how you shine with utter beauty.' This, Abelard, years after he had last seen Héloise. How you shine with utter beauty. Imagine, just imagine, that you could be alive and know that another human being somewhere kept this perception of you in his heart.

Isobel lay on her back in the water with the sun on her body. She felt the warmth of the sun as though it were touching her and she tensed and untensed the muscles in her stomach and her legs as she pushed herself gently through the water on her back. Sometimes she imagined she could picture Abelard himself, severe and merciful in his distant dignity.

She let the cold of the water and the heat of the sun shiver through her.

'Don't like things being out of order, that's all.'

Sam was noisily putting away the dried breakfast plates in his kitchen, his face angry still as it had been all the way back from the village. He had described the events of the morning to the house, although he did not feel that he was explaining everything clearly, because he did not see it all as clearly as he usually did. There were soft, blurred edges to this day when usually everything was bright and defined and set.

'Everything works, we all work together, garden works, house works, Sam works. Everything just right.'

He slammed the cupboard door.

'Breakfast then lunch then tea then bed. Working, painting, looking after things, always a job to do, get it right, get it just right, measure it properly, no surprises. No surprises. Surprises means Sam hasn't planned properly. Shouldn't happen.'

Nothing about the day accorded with Sam's understanding of the world, and he felt unhappy and unsettled about the trip into the village. He felt exposed, as though a light had been turned on him. It was as though he could imagine now looking at himself, it was an awareness which normally would never present itself to him. Now he had an image of himself walking through the village with the girl by his side, and he did not want this image, it intruded on what he would normally see: the house, the bay, the sea, the clouds, his hands working on something.

Now he saw himself from afar as others might see him, and he did not like it.

This was how he had become over the years and it was this lack of self-consciousness, this lack of any awareness, which formed the foundation of his life. His value, his worth, existed only in relation to the things about him with which he interacted, and he had long ago forgotten how he might appear to other people.

The last person he had cared about of course was his mother, with whom he had lived here at the house for the last year of her life. He had vowed to stop working away on the construction sites when she had suffered a fall on the concrete steps down to the beach and she had lain on the sand with a broken, twisted leg for three hours one cold winter morning before someone walking a dog on the beach had spotted her. Sam had returned straight away, incoherent with angry empathy, and had decided never to leave again.

A year later when he was out in the garden tying up the runner bean canes, his mother had been cut down by the stroke and then he was alone. Ten years had passed since then and with every passing of every season which he witnessed with such keen precision and interest, Sam disappeared from himself and was absorbed into the surroundings and the elements of his life.

The arrival of the child today upset this balance. It was different, he knew it was different to when, say, the cat first appeared. The cat arrived and demanded shelter and food, and over the next few years he became an occasional part of Sam's life and they both understood that and accepted it and then life went on quietly.

That was what he feared: the breaking of the silence.

He turned around from the sink but the girl was not there. He looked in the front room where she had slept and his own bedroom, but there was no sign of her. He went back through the kitchen and out into the yard, and found her sitting on the white concrete floor with his fishing line on her lap and her black hair dropped over her face as she bent forwards under the bright hot afternoon sun and worked away with her little fingers at the knots on the line. Sam watched her.

The line was thick and was wrapped around a wooden peg. On one end was attached to it a series of hooks held on by thinner threads. These had become tangled the last time Sam had pulled the line in from his boat on the bay, and he had left the bundle on the ground by the wall and had been planning to unravel it today or tomorrow in preparation for another evening fishing trip when the tides turned.

The girl looked up and saw him. She stood up and handed him the end of the line where the first hooks began, then she walked slowly backwards, feeding out the line which she had untangled, until she reached the wall. She lay the line on the floor and rested a stone on it so that it would remain taut, then she walked back again across the courtyard, slowly feeding out the line and untangling it as she went.

Sam stood still holding the end and thinking, yes, that is how I would do it, lay it all out flat on the floor, no more tangles then. Finally she reached the point on the wooden spindle where the line was clean and not muddled and she began to retrace her steps, rewinding the line onto the spindle until she reached the first of the hooks hanging off their threads, and each one she carefully dug into the thick cork around the handle of the spindle and wound the rest of the line on until she had wound the last hook and line and she was standing back in front of Sam.

He let go of the end and the fishing line was repaired. She handed it back to Sam, and he smiled.

'Come on,' he said. 'We've had a day of it, about time we had something to eat. You must be hungry.'

She looked at him with her solemn little face, her black hair fluttering in the breeze over the collar of her black dress, her feet still in Sam's old brown sandals. He laughed, shaking his head, and she followed him back into the kitchen.

Five

I sobel picked up the postcard from the mantelpiece, turned it over. There was her handwriting. A few rushed sentences, a brief description of a party she had been to with some of the nurses. She remembered writing it only weeks ago. On the mantelpiece in the tiny front room of the house were several other postcards, all instantly recognisable. In the golden early evening light, Isobel stood still and listened to the silent house.

It was cancer, apparently. From initial diagnosis to what the hospital later described as 'a relatively pain-less conclusion' it took only three weeks. The cancer had already torn through her bones and was gnawing at her lungs when she went to see her doctor complaining of an unusual lethargy. And throughout those three weeks, her mother refused to give permission for her daughter, her only relative, to be contacted.

It had been the solicitor handling her Will who had contacted Isobel.

'I am so very sorry,' he had said. 'It was really most unusual. The hospital was very keen to contact you, but of course, these new privacy laws… It is most unfortu-nate. She wished, I believe, to be left in peace.'

Isobel walked over to the window. The carpet was new – her mother had mentioned it in the last postcard she had received, a couple of months ago.

'Dear Isobel. Summer starting now, tourists arriving in droves. I have purchased a new carpet for the lounge. I hope you are well. Your loving mother.'

The windows were covered by lace curtains. Outside, two children were laughing as they walked past. There was dust on the sideboard in front of the window. She picked up a framed photograph. It was the picture she remembered best from childhood: her mother and father's wedding day. Her mother, pretty and dark in a white wedding dress, her father shy beside her in his army uniform. Her mother had kept it in the same place on the sideboard all these years. Beside it, another frame, this time of Isobel, wearing her school uniform. These isolated symbols of a family which, at last, was at an end.

'Only love given freely, rather than the constriction of the marriage tie, is of significance to an ideal relationship.' Isobel remembered writing these words of Héloise in her journal, upstairs in her bedroom, during the dying period of her parents' marriage.

Even with her mother gone, Isobel could feel the disappointment which clung to the walls of this little house, and she put her hands on the sideboard letting it take her weight, as she sank her head and breathed slowly and deliberately. In the quiet of the house, now just the sigh of her breath.

What happened to her parents? How could they live a life of such pettiness, such unhappiness? She recalled them clashing over trivial things, but she had no memory of emotions, of grand declarations or battles. As she grew older, her father insistently confided in his young daughter ('Why, Is, why is she like this? What have I done?'), while her mother grew colder and angrier. Isobel could remember years of silence in this house, broken by a pathetic question from her father which Isobel would have to pretend had been directed to her, as her mother sat ignoring them both and watching the television.

'If you leave,' he had said to Isobel once, as her nights out on the headland became more reckless, and her disregard for village convention more obvious, 'then so will I. I can't stay here without you. With her.' Isobel ignored his threats, paid them no attention; in fact, she despised him for letting her see his misery so close up.

And when finally she left the village, then so did he; and discovered, poor wretch, that now both the women in his life had slipped from his grasp. The sentimental, pleading letters he sent to her at her new address in the city, begging her to forgive him for leaving, asking to meet, were returned. Isobel couldn't, at that age, understand how he could have done it, and she refused all his requests for a meeting. She was oddly severe in her condemnation of his departure, uncharacteristically resolute, and she refused to visit him in the bedsitting room he had taken elsewhere in the city. Of all the people she was drawn to help, she couldn't help him – it was impossible.

A year later, he wrote to her to tell her that he was moving to live with his sister and her family in Australia, and two years after that he was dead.

'You broke his heart,' Isobel's aunt wrote to her. 'Both of you, with your selfishness and your cruelty. You broke his heart.'

She straightened up, closed her eyes and slowly rotated her head. After a minute, she opened them again. She would have to look around.

Nothing much had changed. The kitchen at the back of the little house looked out onto a concrete yard, and some of her mother's washing – a couple of shirts, some underwear, a towel – were still dangling from pegs on the washing line. They must have been there for weeks. Isobel instinctively looked for the back door key, and it was still there, on a hook beside the sink. She went out and collected the washing, and carefully folded each piece into a pile on the draining board.

She went upstairs, where there were two bedrooms. Her parents had had one, she the other. Her mother's room was clean, the bed was made with a pink eiderdown. There was a Bible on the bedside table. She opened the wardrobe, and her mother's clothes were neatly arranged. On the top shelf, there were shoeboxes and bulging carrier bags. Isobel knew she would have to go through all these soon.

Next door, her bedroom was tidy. Her mother must have had it painted recently, the gloss white picture rail gleamed in the evening sunlight. Her bed, where she had lain night after night, reading the volumes she borrowed from the bookshop, was tucked into the corner of the room. There was a dark oak dresser, and some shelves on the wall, which were empty.

Isobel sat on her bed. Her shoes knocked against something solid, and she reached her hand down. Under the bed was a metal trunk. She pulled it out, and opened the lid. Inside it was full of the remnants of her childhood: books, drawings, school exercise books, photographs. All neatly packed away into this grey metal trunk, which she remembered now had been her father's Army packing case. She closed the lid, pushed the case back under the bed. Then she lay down, overwhelmed suddenly with a great tiredness. She closed her eyes for a while.

At the end of the day Sam sat on the bench outside the house and watched the sun set over the western headland. From this bench he could see over the whole wide sweep of the bay, and the beach in the gathering dark was empty now and the sea was once again settled after the rough conditions of the previous day. A few seagulls still soared lazily overhead, and a kestrel hovered, one last prey in sight before the light was lost.

The girl was asleep inside in his mother's bed. He had found an old nightdress in the cupboard which his mother had stitched for him when he was a child, and after she had got into bed he had come back into the dark front room and had placed a candle on the window sill and then had touched her forehead and said gently, 'You get some sleep now, you get some good sleep,' and she had closed her eyes and slept.

Outside on the bench he felt calm again. He had enjoyed the girl's company today. Although she still didn't talk, she seemed to know how to help him without getting in the way, and as he had gone about the tasks of the afternoon she had either been there to hand him tools or clear up, or she had quietly occupied herself with some task of her own. At one point he had found her in the kitchen rearranging the knives and forks and spoons in the cutlery drawer, and later when he was washing up after supper he noticed that she had cleaned inside the kitchen drawers too.

But he was still uneasy in his mind as he sat looking out at the darkening sea. It had been his way for a long time now to be quiet, to look after his own matters, to avoid the attentions of others. His life, with the things around him, and the beach, and the sea, was complete he thought, and somehow he knew that the arrival of the girl had created a change to that balance which was beyond his control.

At the same time he felt that he was happy for her to

be here, and her lack of speech in some ways was com-
forting. She did not seem strange to him, in fact it felt as
though she had been with him for a long time already.
He shook his head.

'We'll see,' he murmured to the bench. 'Take it
slowly.'

It was a warm night, and Sam began to doze himself
out in the twilight as the stars silently appeared over him
and the sea heaved and flowed out in the dark.

Isobel woke up. The room was cold, and the street light
outside shone through the window. She lay on the bed,
and remembered how she used to pretend that the house
was looking out to sea, and the street lamp was the lighthouse at the end of the headland.

She must have been asleep for an hour or more. She
got up and walked into the bathroom next door, splashed
some water on her face. She looked at her face in the
mirror, drops of water falling from her skin back into
the basin.

Back downstairs in the living room, Isobel opened the
cupboards of the sideboard. Her mother always used to
keep a bottle of whisky in the house, she liked one small
glass every evening before she went to bed. She fetched a
glass from the kitchen, and sat down on the sofa, placing
the bottle and the glass on the tiled coffee table.

An hour later, fumbling with the key and unsteady on

her feet, Isobel locked the front door of the house and walked to the end of the street. She turned right at the end and, bumping the wall now and then, she continued until she reached the promenade. She crossed the street, passed the pub which was noisy now with the villagers and the tourists, and held onto the rail as she went down the steps onto the sand of the beach.

The moon sat high over the water, and the surf broke rhythmically on the sand in the dark. Isobel walked slowly down towards the water, her arms now stretched out wide each side, and she laughed as her shoes sank a little into the wet sand of the shore. Another wave broke weakly in front of her, and the sea lapped up around her feet. She stepped back, then turned around, her arms still stretched out, her head leaning back and tears brimming from her closed eyes.

In the moonlight with the slow waves of the evening sea rolling onto the beach, her body swaying and her arms stretched out, she seemed to dance.

Six

S aturday came hot and still again over the village and the great bay.

In the quiet morning air a flock of starlings swirled over the rooftops of the village and then sped up and over the headland, ducking down the cliffs to swoop over Sam's house and then over the rocks of the beach which were revealed by the low tide. In the village it was a working day, because the tourists still had to be catered for, but there was a more tranquil air, as fathers in shorts showing pale hairless legs flip-flopped to the newsagent for the newspapers; children who had been at the village for a few days played on the beach without their parents; mothers lay in beds in the hotel and in guesthouses and rented cottages dozing or reading magazines or novels.

On the beach of the village a young man unlocked the cabin holding the rented deckchairs, and the lifeguards drank coffee in their observation hut and swapped stories from Friday night. The air was filled with the smells of breakfast, and in one of the streets boys' voices echoed as they played football against the church wall.

Up on the headland the first walkers were already keenly marching along the coast path, four of them in shorts and hiking gear having taken an early break-fast and now intent on reaching the next village on the other side of the great bay in time for a pub lunch.

Down by the rocks surrounding the lighthouse at the end of the headland two boys cast out spinning lines from their rods, the silver lures flashing in the morning sunlight as they flew forty or fifty feet out into the water before they were reeled in, swivelling and turning in the water to attract the bass that scoured the rocks for fresh food.

An early morning yacht bent over in the breeze a mile now from the lighthouse and headed due west, three crew relaxed in the cockpit with the hot morning sun on their backs.

On the beach of the great bay, Sam and the girl were crabbing amongst the exposed rocks where they had climbed the day before. The girl was tiny and nimble, and scampered over the rocks ahead of Sam, peering into wet dark gullies, occasionally gesticulating back to him with wide excited eyes, when he would follow and poke about in the rocks where she was pointing with a long iron bar hooked at one end.

In half an hour he already had two good-sized crabs which scrabbled noisily in the black plastic bucket. At one point the girl, impatient with Sam's slow arrival, reached out and grabbed the iron hook from him and launched it into the thin crevice to pull out another wriggling brown crab, and her look of fear and delight and excitement as the crab wrestled to escape the end of the hook made Sam shout with laughter and he leaned over and picked up the angry crab with his thumb and fore-finger as the girl clapped her hands.

'Don't listen to what they tell you about crab meat,' said Sam to the girl a couple of hours later. They were sitting at the kitchen table with the three cooked crabs in front of them, and the girl had looked enquiringly to Sam before touching one of them. 'You can eat just about anything of it, you just don't want to eat these bits here,' he said, pointing a thick finger at the soft tissue under the front of the shell. 'But they won't kill you, just don't taste right. Leave them, eat the rest, like this.'

The girl watched him with serious attention as he dug his fork into the flesh of the crab, then she did the same and tasted her first mouthful and she swallowed it and grinned at him.

'Good isn't it?' he said.

He watched her while she explored the crab, dug out chunks of flesh and ate them. Her hair fell down over her face sometimes as she ate. She flicked it back, keen to carry on with the meal.

'Won't be many crabs left on the beach if she eats like that,' he said to the kitchen.

He liked to see her eat so well. He only ate crabs at the weekend, as a treat. He knew that if you over-fished the low tide pools, you would put too much pressure on the crab and the numbers and sizes would begin to reduce.

He ate more himself. It was a rhythm, everything was a rhythm. He liked the way the girl fitted in with the rhythm of his life. His awareness of time was broad and seasonal, and yesterday's uncomfortable trip could have been years ago now. And although the girl did not speak, he enjoyed her attention when he explained things to her, and he loved to see the way her little black eyes expressed so vividly her fear or her pleasure or her excitement. Her strange arrival was already of less interest to him.

'Got another mouth to feed now,' he said to the fridge as he put away the butter and milk after their lunch. 'Better go back into the village this afternoon, get more bread and milk.'

The girl scraped the last few scraps of flesh from the crab shells and took them out into the yard to lay them on the wall for the seagulls. Sam came out with her, and hurled the empty shells over the wall; they clattered down the edge of the cliff to land on the beach below at the foot of the steps to the house.

He looked at her.

'Good,' he said. 'Good.'

By ten o'clock in the morning, Isobel had already checked out of the hotel.

She had woken early again, with a dry headache to remind her of last night on the beach, and realised straight away that it made sense to move into her mother's house while she was here. She would save money on the hotel bill, and she would be able to take her time going through her mother's effects. And despite the headache, she had woken too with a strange sense of optimism, a feeling unusual for her that life could present clear possibilities, real options. She had brought her assorted notes about the book she wanted to write, the book about Abelard and Héloise, and one of her first thoughts that morning was that she could work on it on the dining table in the room her mother never used between the living room and the kitchen. She had taken a week off work at the hospital: why didn't she use that time to do something positive, something real?

And now here she is in the dining room, and once more she finds herself pausing over Héloise's words in her first letter to Abelard:

'I would have had no hesitation, God knows, in following you or going ahead at your bidding to the flames of Hell. My heart was not in me but with you, and now, even more, if it is not with you it is nowhere; truly without you it cannot exist.'

My heart was not in me. This phrase had been locked in Isobel's mind for so long, only now it seemed to take on a clearer meaning. If not inside her, then where had her heart lain all these years? The years spent in the city, looking after people, listening to people's problems, watching people go by in the parks – had she, without knowing, let her heart settle somewhere a long time ago, somewhere amongst the dust and the shafts of sunlight and the shelves and the quiet sanctuary of the bookshop?

In the silence of her mother's house she looked back over the years. Where had they gone?

The doorbell rang. Isobel started. She paused for a moment, then got up and walked to the front door.

She opened the door to find a woman of about her age, with hennaed hair, a long skirt, and a brown face with lines that spoke of children and the sea. Isobel said, 'Hello? Can I help you?'

'You don't remember me, do you Isobel?' the woman said. 'I'm Marion.'

Immediately, Isobel remembered her old school friend, the dreamy teenager who had accompanied her on some of the illicit moonlight walks to the lighthouse with boys. They hadn't spoken for fifteen years or more.

'I live opposite,' she said, nodding her head back. 'I saw you arrive this morning. I'm so sorry. I so wanted to contact you, but I didn't know where you lived, and your mother...'

Isobel smiled.

'It's all right. I know. She didn't want me to know. I understand.'

'I couldn't understand. I couldn't understand, but she was so sure. She was so sure about everything. I wanted to find you, but...'

They hugged, Isobel feeling a little awkward. She

couldn't remember now how close they had been. She was apprehensive about the intrusion, but the woman seemed upset.

'Come in, please, come in.'

They sat in the living room, and the woman immediately began to tell Isobel how she had tried to persuade her mother to let her contact her daughter, but to no avail.

'I sort of looked out for her, you see,' Marion said, looking up to Isobel with a worried frown, and Isobel thought, this is all the life that carried on while I was away. This is what was happening here. She felt suddenly quite cold about it.

'She was very independent, you know how she was,' the woman continued. 'She was so very proud of you, though. Your postcards, she would always read out your postcards.' She shook her head. 'I never really understood why you never came home. She said you were caught up in your work, or something.'

Isobel smiled.

'I said that she should have told you then about her being ill, but she said that she didn't want to worry you. She said that she'd be out of the hospital at the end of the week.'

There were tears now in Marion's eyes. Isobel could feel herself becoming brittle with irritation. But it wasn't this woman's fault. She was kindly. They had been friends.

'Listen,' she said. 'Please don't be upset. Let me make you a cup of coffee. You stay here for a moment, I need to get some milk from the shop. I won't be a minute.'

There was a little supermarket in the next street, and Isobel needed to escape for a moment, to get some air.

'I'll be right back.'

'Come on you, we need more bread and milk. Eating us out, you are!'

Sam and the girl set off again up the steep path from the house to the top of the headland. She'll need more clothes though, Sam thought, as he looked at her ahead of him in her little black dress and his old brown sandals. He would look through the cupboards thoroughly when he got back and see which of his childhood clothes his mother had stored would fit her. He might have to get her more shoes though, as the mend he had made on the sandals would only be temporary.

There was nobody at the top of the headland on the path this time, and they stopped at the bench and waited for the falcon to appear down below in the cliff edges. While they waited Sam pointed out the birds: how to spot the difference between the common gull and the herring gull ('common gull, he's a bit fatter, not so long, and his beak is more green, and he doesn't glide so long as the herring gull, he's lazy about flapping his wings, the herring gull') and how to tell the sandpipers apart ('there's one, you see, that hovers over the water like that down there, and there's another and I can't remember his name now but he likes to sit straight in the water, no messing about').

The girl followed his lessons intently, sometimes standing up to get a better view down to the water at the foot of the cliffs. Then Sam saw the falcon emerge as though in slow motion from its hiding place on a cliff edge and he pointed it out to the girl, and they both admired it as it flew calmly across the front of the cliffs.

'King, he is, king of the predators, he rules this cliff,' said Sam and they both watched respectfully.

After a while they got up and carried on to the road which led down into the village. Sam had put out of his mind any plans to find the girl's parents, and for him this was just another shopping trip. This was how he was, how Sam always was.

They walked along the promenade and turned down the first side street off the main road where the village supermarket was. Inside it was busy with holidaymakers still, some padding up and down the five aisles in swimming costumes and beach shoes. He found milk and bread, then led the girl to the small beach clothes section at the back of the store. There was a rack of rubber beach shoes, and he picked out a pair of pink shoes and handed them down to her.

'See if they fit then, have them in case old Sam's shoes give out.'

The girl took them so carefully as though they might break, and she looked up at Sam and he nodded, and she undid one of her sandals and replaced it with the bright pink rubber shoe. Sam bent his huge body down over her and prodded at the end of the shoe with his forefinger.

'Got enough space there?'

She nodded, then took the shoe off again and put her brown sandal back on and Sam led her to the cash tills, holding his milk and bread and the tiny pair of pink shoes.

They waited in line while a family was served, then Sam passed the items to the young woman sat at the cash till, who passed each of them over an electronic scanner which bleeped several times. The woman stared dully at the green figures on the cash machine reader and read them out without looking up at Sam.

'No, that's wrong,' Sam said, not to the woman but leaning over towards the cash register. He was smiling and was speaking gently. 'No, you got that wrong. I thought I heard you bleeping too much, you bleeped too much.'

The woman looked up at him irritated, and repeated the total she had first said.

'Don't matter what she says,' Sam said to the cash machine, still smiling. 'You know you counted up wrong. You counted two bottles of milk, I heard you.'

There was already a small queue behind Sam and the

girl, and he continued to smile patiently at the machine, and the girl put her hand in his and smiled up at him too.

The woman at the till stared at Sam.

'Are you trying to be funny or something?'

At that moment an older woman who was the supervisor came over and said, 'Anything wrong here?'

Sam leaned over and pointed at the green figures on the display.

'You know you've added up wrong, better check your figures again, can't go making mistakes like that.'

The woman seated at the till stood up quickly.

'Don't touch me!' she yelled.

'Calm down, calm down,' said the supervisor. She looked at Sam who was still waiting patiently for the machine to admit its mistake, then she jabbed a finger at a button on the machine and a receipt printed out which she tore off and examined.

'I'm so sorry sir,' she said to Sam. 'It looks as though your milk was read twice, you're quite right. Susan, please pass this gentleman's goods through once more.'

The young woman sat down again and grabbed Sam's purchases, passed them over the electronic reader, and read out an altered price in a sullen monotone.

Sam was chuckling, and he said to the child as she carefully placed the pink shoes into a carrier bag with the milk and the bread,

'Machine forgot how to add up!'

Oblivious to the angry way in which the woman thrust his change into his hand – throughout the whole incident Sam avoided any eye contact with anyone apart from the child – Sam put the change in his pocket and the unlikely pair, the huge man and the tiny girl, walked hand in hand out of the shop.

The next customer in the queue placed a pint of milk on the counter.

'Bit of a character,' Isobel said to the cashier as she handed over some money.

'Bloody nutter, that's who he is,' the woman replied, her voice full of indignation. 'Bloody village nutter, gives me the spooks. Bloody weirdo. And who in their right mind would trust a kid like that with him? Everyone knows he's not right in the head, gives me the creeps. A kid like that as well.'

Isobel stared at the backs of Sam and the child as they went through the doors of the supermarket, and just at that moment the child, still holding Sam's hand, turned her head and looked straight back at Isobel and she continued to stare through the window until they turned the corner and were gone.

On impulse, Isobel grabbed her change and the milk, and ran out after them. They were already halfway down the street, and the child had turned her head to the front again. Isobel ran after them.

'Excuse me!' she called out, brushing past a family on the pavement. 'Excuse me, hold on a second please!'

Sam continued to walk, but the child turned her head once more to stare at Isobel. Sam was thinking about the cash register, and was still chuckling over it.

Isobel reached them, and she tapped Sam on the shoulder.

'Excuse me, would you mind if I asked you something?'

Sam stopped, turned around, but did not look straight at Isobel. He looked just past her, back down the street. He had a strange smile on his face.

'My name is Isobel, and I remember seeing you yesterday in the crowd at the beach, and you said something, something about things not being right. I just wondered what you meant.'

Sam looked at the supermarket sign at the end of the road, and then he looked up at the sky. He squeezed the little girl's hand tight.

'We must go now,' he said. 'We have things that must be done.'

Still with his gentle smile, he turned, and the two of them continued their walk to the end of the street. They turned left at the end towards the promenade and the steep hill out of the village.

Seven

With an all-too familiar sense of empathy, Isobel re-established some form of relationship with her old schoolfriend back at her mother's house. She listened to her, sipping coffee from her mother's cup. Marion was married to a local fisherman called Michael, she had three children, and she had lived in the house opposite for nine years now. After an hour, and just as Isobel was beginning to flag, Marion looked up at her again with that concerned crease on her brow, and she said:

'But what happened to you Isobel? You just disappeared. We used to talk about you, you know. In the pub. We'd wonder where you'd gone. And then after a few years, well, we just stopped talking about you. It was only me, living here opposite your mum, and every so often checking in on her. She was very private, but she would always mention you. And that was all I ever heard of you. Why did you just disappear like that?'

'Oh,' Isobel replied, looking away. 'I didn't really. It just didn't occur to me to come back.' Was that true? If it was or it wasn't, what did it matter now?

Then a few minutes later, Isobel heard herself accepting

an invitation to supper that evening with Marion and her husband. Christ almighty, she thought, and for a second she imagined her mother – tall and rigid, in the thick coat she wore in summer as in winter – nodding her head with a sneer, as though to say, that'll teach you. That'll teach you.

And a few hours later, she found herself in the garden across the road, with Marion and her husband, a taciturn man with longish, greying hair. All three children were out with friends in the village, and they were sitting on white plastic chairs in the little patch of grass, empty plates on the table between them. Isobel had brought two bottles of wine, and Marion was a little drunk.

'It just seems so sad, her ending her days on her own like that. So sad. I mean, I don't mean that you didn't care for her, I don't mean that, it's just so sad.'

'Yes.'

'And she kept that little house so clean, and she'd never let me help her, not even carry her shopping. If I invited her in for a coffee, she'd never come, but she was always so polite. I don't know.'

Isobel thought of her mother, grim in her thick coat, sitting in that front room.

'She was always nice to the kids though, wasn't she Michael? Always giving them sweets, which she wasn't supposed to, but she seemed to like to do it. I didn't want to say anything. Oh dear.'

And Isobel thought too of Héloise, abbess of Paraclete,

re-reading Abelard's letters alone in her room. Taking comfort from them, while the women of the abbey went about their duties in silence. Then her mother again, sitting in her armchair, re-reading the wretched post-cards she had sent her.

'What do you think, Isobel? Do you think she was happy, your mother? I always hoped she was. Do you think she was?'

Isobel didn't really hear, and the garden was quiet.

Michael opened his eyes, and looked at Isobel.

'Listen,' he said, his voice gentler than it had been. 'It's been a long day for Isobel, Marion. We should let her get some rest.'

Marion was still frowning, and Isobel could feel the sympathy flowing across the table from her like a virus. She shook herself, then remembered the incident in the afternoon.

'Oh, I know what I was going to ask you. Do you know a very tall, strong-looking man with a little grand-daughter?' And she told them about the encounter in the supermarket.

Michael looked at his wife, then back at Isobel.

'Yes, I know him. Everyone knows him here. He's called Sam. Why?'

'Nothing really. I'm just intrigued by the way that little girl stares at me.'

Again, an awkward silence. Michael coughed.

'Sam, he lives in that little cottage over on the other

side of the headland. The one with the flat roof, that used to be the lighthouse before they built the new one.'

Isobel smiled.

'Oh, I know it, I was looking at it from the sea yesterday. It used to belong to an old woman, she used to clean for Mum sometimes. I used to know her.'

'Sam's Mum,' said Michael. 'She died years ago. He came back to the village to look after her when she was ill and he's lived there on his own ever since.'

'He came back to look after his mother?'

'His dad was killed on the lifeboats when he was a lad.'

'Oh.'

'He's a bit of a loner. They say he was a bit of a fighter when he was younger. You kept away from him, the older lads on the boat say.'

'But what about this girl?' Marion re-joined the conversation. 'I never knew old Sam had any relatives.'

'Well, he hasn't, has he?' her husband replied sharply. 'Of course he hasn't, not Sam.'

'But –'

'No-one knows,' he cut in. 'In the pub last night, old Geoff, he was talking about it. He said he'd seen Sam in the village yesterday with this little girl, just sitting on the bench over on the main street. Said he was just sitting there reading the newspaper, this little girl next to him. Geoff said he went up to them and Sam's off straight away and he says the two of them walked off hand in hand back up the hill. Old Geoff says he's never see anything like it.'

'Who can it be though?' cried Marion. 'It doesn't seem right. A little kiddie you say? No, that can't be right.'

'Now what do you know about it?' Michael turned his face to his wife. 'It's just village gossip.'

'What is?' asked Isobel.

Marion looked at her. 'Don't you remember Sam at all, Isobel? Don't you remember when we were at school, and sometimes we would have dares to go over to spy on his house when he was back on holiday with his mother? Don't you remember? We used to call him the bogeyman!'

'I don't remember that. Are you sure?'

'Oh I don't know, it all just seems wrong to me,' said Marion. She sighed. 'A little kiddie.' She looked up at Isobel, her frown returned. 'That's not right, is it?'

'Stupid talk,' said Michael. 'Let's leave it. It's late.'

For a second Michael looked at Isobel, and the way he looked at that moment and the drunken confusion on Marion's face and the still golden evening light all seemed to stay absolutely in place as though Isobel were watching a film, and just for a second she imagined herself leaning over to Marion and whispering in Marion's ear, 'I am going to sleep with your husband,' and Marion nodding absently, still thinking about the little girl. For that second, Isobel's heart missed a beat, and she knew that this was one of those moments when the secrecy of life was revealed. Just for a moment, the clutter departed, and there was a still certainty, like one of the casts her sculptor made.

Marion and Michael began to rise from their seats.

'Time to round up the kids,' Marion said sleepily.

Isobel was aware of the wine, but she was convinced that for just that second in the garden the thought had existed, had taken concrete form, of Isobel and Michael making love. She had no interest in him, it was the moment which she was concentrating on. These moments she treasured, as though they were waypoints in her life.

'That was lovely,' she said, yawning. 'It was so nice of you to invite me over.'

A little later, she lay in her old bed with the curtains open, in the moonlight. She lay awake for some time, listening to noises in the village, front doors slamming, cars parking. She noticed an old poster of a pop star she had pinned to the back of the bedroom door twenty years ago. The breeze flapped the curtains and outside the moon shone in glittering fragments all over the bay of the village and cast a shadow over the peak of the headland down to Sam's house where the child lay still and quiet and sleeping in the old cot in the front room, her new pair of pink rubber shoes laid neatly beside her head on the pillow, and in his bedroom Sam slept profoundly.

Eight

Sam's mother was called Bethany, and after the death of his father when so many things were swirling about in the mind of the little four-year-old boy, he mixed up some of the early general knowledge lessons from the village infant school with the exotic sound of his mother's name amidst the Annes and Janes and Marys of the village, and he convinced himself that the spread of rocks at the foot of the concrete steps leading down from the house to the beach was a foreign country where his mother had been born.

For months after her husband's death, Sam's mother would call for her boy in the house to no avail, and eventually she would find him all the way down at the bottom of the steps, playing quietly in the sand and the rocks, unaware always that to him this was a foreign country which he had reached with some difficulty by clambering down the steep concrete steps. She could not understand why he kept returning, but even as an adult Sam could recall the mixture of adventure and security which these trips to what he thought was the country of his mother's birth represented to him.

He remembered this again as he descended the steps behind the child. They had finished breakfast, cleared up and Sam had examined the state of the sea while the girl threw breadcrumbs at the seagulls by the wall of the house. The tide had turned and there were strong currents following the curve of the bay, and Sam had seen some agitation amongst the gulls and the oyster catchers.

'Looks like the bass are feeding,' he said, only this morning he turned his head specifically to address the girl. He was not talking to the house.

She looked at him hopefully.

'Think we could try that line out that you fixed yesterday, take it out on the boat and see if we can catch some supper.'

The girl's eyes were bright with excitement, and once they had gathered the line and a bucket and the oars and rollocks he had let the child lead the way down the steep steps to the beach.

At the foot of the steps stood Isobel.

She had woken early again this morning, and had felt out of place in the little bedroom. The dawn light had streamed through the window, and she had wanted to get out of the house. She knew she should have been sorting out her mother's things, but she thought first of Sam and the girl, and she remembered how the girl had stared at her, twice now. Why did she stare? She would go for a walk over to the big beach via the headland on the coast path, wait on the beach to see if she could spot them.

She had been on the beach for an hour, a fleece over her to keep her warm until the sun made it over the headland. Her determination was beginning to waver, and a sense of feeling ridiculous pacing an empty beach on her own on a Sunday morning was beginning to take hold, when she caught sight of the little girl, still wearing the odd black dress, leading the giant of a man down the stairs.

The sun was way over the headland now, and Isobel could see them clearly in the bright morning light, and could see the man was carrying two long wooden oars over his shoulder. She walked towards the steps to meet them as they reached the beach.

'Hello,' she said, directly to Sam, 'are you Sam? My name is Isobel. I knew your mother.'

Sam had not noticed her on the way down as his mind had taken him back to when he was the size of the child in front of him and he used to shelter down here in what he thought was a foreign land.

When he saw Isobel now, he recognised the blonde young woman who had been sitting on the bench on the coast path the other morning. He was caught unprepared. The child had stopped beside him and was looking out to sea. The beach was empty and the tide was about half way up, coming in.

'Oh,' he said.

Then he said, 'I was just thinking about her.'

'She used to clean for my mother in the village, and sometimes she would invite me to her house and she would give me delicious teas.'

'Ah,' said Sam.

The image in his mind of his mother waiting in the kitchen with the slice of bread and the mug of tea for him was very clear, and he tried to imagine her serving a bigger spread to this person while he had been away working. She must have had to be nice to the child if she worked for her mother. His mother could easily make some nice buns, or a cake, or some jam sandwiches.

He felt a pang of sadness as he thought of his mother having to prepare such a meal as well as having to toil all day cleaning houses.

'Yes, she was a good woman,' said Sam, and he looked down at the child. 'She would have made you tea too, you know!' and at this thought he felt cheerful. He looked at Isobel, not half-glancing but straight at her this time.

'I'm on holiday,' said Isobel, smiling. 'I was having an early morning walk and I noticed the house and remembered your mother being so kind.'

'Well she's gone now, ten years,' said Sam. 'Thank you for remembering her so well.'

He moved off, and the child walked beside him. He felt his life changing. It unsettled him, he was unsure about this direct human contact. He looked down at the child. Since her arrival, his life had changed, and he was uncertain what this meant. 'It's like it's a different life,' he said to the child, and she looked up at him without showing any emotion in her face.

'I suppose it must seem a long time ago.' Isobel had followed them as they had begun to walk along the beach. 'Since your mother passed away.'

Sam turned to look at her again, and Isobel drew up so she was walking alongside them.

'You *are* Sam, aren't you?'

He continued walking ahead, the child at his side.

'She used to speak about you when I had tea with her, but I never met you. I think you were living away or something. I was still at school. She used to be so proud of you, she would always talk about you.'

Sam felt a flush of emotion, and he squeezed the child's hand that he was holding. The little girl was still looking up at him.

'She was brave,' he said. 'She lived here on her own for years and she never complained and she never had a bad word to say about anyone.' He lifted his chin up and clenched his jaw and felt a flutter inside him and looked back at the young woman. 'You knew her then?'

'Well, I got to know her a little. I used to love coming over to the house for one of her teas. It was like a special treat that no-one else knew about. My mum didn't even know I came over, because I just liked it being a secret treat. I used to sit and eat and she would tell me about you and about things about the beach. She used to know so much.'

Sam closed his eyes just for a second as they all three walked along the beach, and as he did so Isobel looked down at the child who was the other side of Sam and saw that the little girl was once again staring straight at her. Isobel thought: is it you? Is it you who has brought me here? Did you make me come?

'Well, she knew all about this beach,' said Sam, opening his eyes.

They were walking along the shoreline towards the centre of the bay, and once more the sun was already hot behind them. To the right a family had appeared on the beach and were setting out towels and buckets and spades and surfboards. The sky was blue and cloudless. A white double decker bus drove along the cliff road up in the distance and far ahead on the sand a flock of oyster catchers paddled in the shallow water pecking at the mussels on the rocks.

'She taught me most of what I know about it, she lived here all her life.'

'Oh yes,' said Isobel. 'She was always so knowledgeable.'

'I miss her really,' said Sam, looking into the distance. 'Didn't have enough time with her. Never thought she'd go so soon like that. Never thought it.'

'It must have made you very sad.'

Sam looked at Isobel.

'Yes,' he said. 'It made me very sad.'

The child was still looking past Sam up at Isobel. Isobel smiled at her.

'But it looks like you have your hands full now,' she said brightly. 'What a pretty little girl. She must keep you lively.'

Sam looked down at the child, then back to Isobel again.

'Oh she does! She keeps old Sam lively. I'd say she does.' And suddenly he laughed, but the child did not respond and now stared straight ahead. 'She doesn't say anything, but she's good company.' He was beaming now. 'Yes, she keeps me lively.'

Isobel looked at the child again. 'What pretty hair, and such deep dark eyes. So pretty.'

'Pretty now, you hear that?' said Sam to the child. 'Weren't so pretty when we found you, were you?'

'When you found her?'

'Yes, not so pretty then. Oh no!'

He laughed again. They had reached the collection of boats, and he laid down the oars from his shoulder onto the sand and took the bucket from the child. He took out the rollocks from the bucket and leaned over to fit them on the boat.

'You're off fishing then?' asked Isobel. She wanted to ask if she could join them, but something made her hesitate.

'Yes. Fishing.'

'Would you mind awfully much if I came to call on

you at the house? It would be so lovely to see it again.'

Sam looked up from the boat. The child was staring hard at him now but he did not notice.

'You'd like to see my house?'

'It would be such a treat.'

'Well, I suppose so.'

'I could come this afternoon, about four o'clock, when I always used to come.'

'About four o'clock?'

'Yes, that's when I used to come.'

'Today?'

'Only if you didn't mind.'

'All right then.'

'Oh. That would be lovely. But I mustn't keep you both from your fishing. It's such a lovely day.'

The boat was on a pair of wheels with a rope attached, and Sam pulled it down to the water and heaved it off the cradle, then took the wheels back up the beach beyond where the incoming tide would be able to reach them. Isobel watched the little girl walking beside Sam, first down to the water then back up again with the wheels. As they turned now to go back to the boat, Isobel came with them. The child was carrying the bucket which held the fishing line.

'Would you mind if I took a picture of you and the boat? Your mother always said what a good fisherman you were.'

She pulled out a disposable camera from her bag, and

104

took a picture of a tall, brown faced man with sandy hair and a barrel of a chest, looking surprised at the camera, and beside him holding his hand and in the other holding a black plastic bucket, a tiny little dark-haired girl in a black dress looking at the camera with a stony, expressionless face. In the background was a short wooden boat with its keel resting on the sand in the shallows of the water.

'Thanks,' said Isobel. 'See you later. Good luck!'

They rowed for half an hour in silence out into the middle of the bay, then Sam pulled in the oars and let the boat drift in the gentle current while he looked into what he had packed into the black bucket. There was one other fishing boat out in the bay, a quiet diesel with two men on board slowly trawling up and down the width of the bay. The seagulls were still circling overhead. Back at the shore one or two people were now in the water, and occasionally their shouts or laughs would reach over the surface of the water to break the silence out where the boat was.

'We'll lay your line down on the seabed, see if we can get some turbot,' he said. 'You ready?'

The girl smiled at him.

'First we lay the end of your line down with a weight on the end. I'll do that, don't want you getting your fingers caught.'

But the girl had already taken the fat spindle and had begun lowering the line over the side, letting the metal weight Sam had attached earlier drop into the water first.

'Well, all right, but what are you going to put on those hooks?'

When the first hook appeared, the girl stopped unrolling the line. She reached into the bucket and broke off a piece of bread from the half a loaf which Sam had left soaking in the can of fish oil he kept in a tin outside the front door. Carefully, she threaded it onto the hook, squeezed it tight into place, then lowered the baited hook down into the water. She looked up at Sam and nodded.

He laughed. 'I might have known,' he said. 'All right.'

He took up the oars and pulled two easy strokes, and the girl continued to let out the line until the next hook appeared, and she motioned to Sam with her hand and he pushed the oars back the other way into the water to stop the boat. He waited while she repeated the baiting process, let the second hook over the side and then motioned to Sam again, and he pulled on the oars once more.

Slowly they let out sixteen or seventeen hooks baited with the perfumed bread. When she reached the end of the line and Sam stopped the boat again, she tied the line to the empty plastic milk carton that he had put in the bottom of the bucket, her tiny fingers quickly wrapping the line around the handle of the carton. She let this

106

go onto the water and it floated on the surface. Down below the baited hooks lay on the sand, shifting slowly with the tide.

'It's nice out here this morning, shall we just wait out here for an hour, see what you've got?'

The girl smiled at him again, then she lay down on the stern bench where she had been working from and curled up and closed her eyes under the bright sun of the morning.

'Done a good job there,' said Sam, and she smiled again with her eyes still closed.

So many times he had carried out this task on his own over the years. He had always enjoyed it, enjoyed the precision of the operation, enjoyed the knowledge of the line sitting down below him on the sand. He loved sitting on the boat waiting for the fish to take, looking back at the sweep of the cliffs around the bay as the boat drifted and picking out the different colours of the heather on the cliffs and greeting the seagulls and cormorants and butterflies and crows and starlings who would pass by. He loved the feel of the weight of the water cradling the little wooden boat. He loved the pure long line of the horizon.

And now he had someone else here sharing the whole experience with him.

He thought now how things had changed since she arrived. He was less and less speaking to the familiar components of his life and more now talking directly to the girl. It was not that he deemed the boat, the house, the cooker any less deserving of his time and his thoughts, it was just that his words more naturally seemed to direct themselves to the girl. Even though she did not speak, he knew that she understood everything he said, and he enjoyed telling her about everything. But at the same time, he felt nervous of this change.

She was asleep now at the stern of the boat, her black dress draped over her little body. But she must have some more clothes, he thought. Then he thought: maybe that woman could help choose some? He wouldn't know what clothes a little girl was supposed to have, but that woman looked smart, she'd be able to help them.

He had liked the way she had spoken about his mother. A few people had talked to him after the funeral, but he had really drifted away from people after that and so he had never heard someone else's view of his mother. It was precious to him, this image which Isobel had given him this morning, and he smiled now at the thought of his mother chattering to a little blonde schoolgirl about her day. She must have liked the company, he thought, with him being away so much.

She would have liked the little girl too, he thought. And he was happy that he had these stronger images of his mother now, and he was pleased that his world now accommodated this funny little girl, in her black dress, which he must replace. He looked out over the water which was still today, the surface just sparkling in the sunlight, no crests or swells to disturb the tranquility. A gull flashed low over the surface, and the water lapped gently against the side of the wooden boat.

Nine

Isobel sat in the little dining room. In front of her, on the table, amongst all her old notes about the book, lay a pile of letters. She had found them in a box underneath her mother's bed. What was she supposed to do? She had to look through everything, it was why she was here.

Now, she read letter after letter from her father to her mother, written before she was born. Clumsy, misspelt, with a child-like hand which now she recalled. Every letter overflowing with passion, yearning, desire. Her mother must have kept these letters for forty years, some of them written on Army airmail paper while her father had been stationed abroad. They described two people she had never met.

Her father, when his Service had ended, had moved to the village with her mother to set up a post office, which they had run for twenty years together, before his departure. He had learned about forms and systems in the Army, had been good at it, and the switch from being a corporal in the Ordnance Corps, ordering blankets and food and bullets, to a postmaster in a seaside village – well, it must have worked for a while. Isobel could remember them both behind the counter, her mother sitting on a padded stool counting out money in exchange for pension slips, her father tying up grey bags of post to be collected by the van every day at five o'clock.

She supposed now that she just wouldn't have understood then how their relationship was disintegrating in the claustrophobic atmosphere of the little shop, one street back from the promenade and from the bookshop where she was to work later on. How he had discovered a great emptiness in his soul after the years abroad with the Army, an emptiness he persisted in describing to Isobel once she was old enough to listen. How he tried to keep alive the love that he had felt for her mother when he wrote these letters, how the months and the years passed and his mother's grim determination finally shut him out completely.

Isobel never heard her mother's side of the story. In all the arguments they were to have later, her mother never told her how she had felt when she discovered that her happiness was slipping through her fingers.

'*My darling, my darling,*' she read, gripping the sheet of foolscap on which her father had written. '*It won't be long now my love, and we will be together, properly together as man and wife. I think about this every night, and every day as I work at my desk, I think of you and how beautiful you are and how I am so lucky that you love me like you do.*'

On and on they went, letter after letter. Her mother,

she supposed, must have felt jealous of Isobel, watching her chattering to her father about her day at school as she pegged out washing, cleaned dishes, ironed shirt collars. By the time she was twelve, her mother and father barely communicated, the routine of the post office allowing them to work side by side, day after day, in silence.

From these letters, which now she folded back into the tin petty cash box, to that awful silence, and then to his absurd departure to live in a bed-sitting room. And then Australia. Did he think he might find something again, on the other side of the world? She remembered having to come home and tell her mother about his emigration, which she had heard about in a final letter from him.

'*Dearest Isobel,*' he had written. She could remember it exactly. '*There is nothing left for me here any more. I am moving to Australia, my sister and her husband have invited me to live with them and their family. I can start again there perhaps. Please tell your mother. I want nothing from her or the shop, tell her. I am sorry, so very sorry about everything. Your father.*'

When she read this to her mother, downstairs in the living room, her mother stayed still in her chair for some time, staring at the window, her hands rigid on the arms of the seat. Isobel could see her knuckles gripping the wood tightly. And then her mother turned to her after a while, and said:

'I hope you're happy now.'

That was all. Why did she suppose that she would be happy? She didn't really hope she was happy. Perhaps that was how she had to see it. Perhaps she had to imagine the world conspiring against her, turning the once pretty and light-footed young woman who used to love to dress up in cotton skirts and go dancing with the handsome young Army soldier, into a fierce and rigid character, a silent witness, a martyr.

Isobel would never know. She closed the lid of the tin box. It was time to walk over to the bay again, for her tea. She closed her eyes for a moment, her hands on the table top. She would never know.

At four o'clock, Isobel sat at the long kitchen table in Sam's house, smiling and listening as he described the fishing trip. The sun was still shining strong through the kitchen window, although there was a bank of white cloud building in the sky over the far headland of the great bay.

'Caught us a couple of turbot, didn't you?' he was saying to the child who sat opposite Isobel.

The girl looked up at Sam pleased, then looked at Isobel.

'Look, I'll show you,' he said. And he reached down into the fridge and took out a plate with two thin strips of white turbot skin, lying on top of each other. He had saved these for the cat.

'Ate them for our lunch, didn't we? Good size,' he

said, nodding to the child again. 'Pulled them in herself, didn't you? Pulled them off the hook, snap, broke their necks, broke their necks with those little fingers, look.'

And he beamed towards the child, and Isobel looked at her staring back emotionlessly across the table, and for a second had a vivid image of the little girl calmly snapping the neck of the strong, wriggling fish, and then it lying limp and cold and dead in her hands.

Isobel forced herself to laugh.

'So she's the fisherman of the family, is she? And all the time your mother was telling me it was you – or has she inherited your fishing skills?'

Sam looked at them both.

'I don't know about that,' he said. 'But she knows what she's doing all right, don't you?'

He turned back and began collecting plates to lay out on the table.

'This won't be much of a tea compared with what you said mother made you. But we had a go – made us some buns this afternoon, didn't we?'

The girl smiled up at him again as he brought over a plate with still warm buns on it.

'Mother taught me a few things, so we can put together a bit of tea when we need to.'

Isobel looked around the room, which smelled warm and comfortingly of baking. It was a practical room, she could see how it suited the big man: everything was neat and tidy, saucepans stacked up on a shelf above the worktop, cupboards arranged below. There were no unnecessary objects, no pictures or flowers or scribbled notes. She thought of her own kitchen back home, cluttered with jars and papers and books, and she realised that she felt relaxed in the quiet emptiness of this room. The stone floor under her feet was clean and cool.

Sam laid out cups on the table, and then Isobel saw a black cat step softly into the kitchen through the door which was open to the outside yard.

'Hello,' said Sam, 'more visitors? You've seen them clouds building up, haven't you? Think there's rain coming, thought you'd miss it this time, did you?'

He turned his head to look out of the kitchen window, and Isobel followed his gaze to see the clouds which had been banking up earlier now spreading over the whole bay. She realised that the room had darkened since she had arrived, the clouds had reached the point where the sun was and had blocked it out.

'You'd better eat this turbot skin,' said Sam. 'Saved it for you, didn't we?' He cut up the skin and laid the plate down on the floor, and the cat began to eat.

'What a lovely cat,' she said. 'Yours?'

'Mine? If he's mine, then I'm his. He comes here to get away from the rain, has a bit of my food. He catches a few mice for me.' Sam turned back and began to pour the tea. 'We all get along.'

'It's so nice of you to let me see the house again. I can remember it so well.'

'Ah, you won't remember the fridge, though,' he said, nodding towards the corner. 'Mother wouldn't have bothered with that.'

'No, of course, that wasn't there. But everything else....'

She looked around again. The door into the rest of the house was shut.

'Don't fix things that aren't broke, that's what I think. Let everything do its job, everything gets along all right then. Don't change things that don't need it.'

Isobel was struck by the words. Don't change.

'You are both very lucky to live in such a beautiful place.' She was surprised at how emotional her voice sounded when she said that.

Sam looked at her. 'Thank you for coming and having tea with mother. She must have liked your visits. I left her on her own all those years, earning money. Must have been lonely for her. Glad she had someone to talk to every now and then. I see it now this little monkey is here – nice having someone to talk to a bit.'

Sam looked at the little girl, who was munching though her second bun, and she looked back with her little dark eyes wide as she crammed the food into her mouth, as though she had been caught in the act, and both Sam and Isobel laughed.

'What's her name?' Isobel asked.

Sam stopped laughing, looked seriously at the girl, then looked back at Isobel. 'I don't know.'

Isobel was still smiling. 'What do you mean?'

'I mean I don't know her name. She hasn't told me. She doesn't talk.'

'But...'

Sam thought for a moment. The little girl ducked down below the table to give a piece of bun to the cat who had finished the fish and was sitting patiently by her feet on the stone floor.

Sam looked at Isobel. It was so strange for him, looking at someone. She was wearing a pretty summer dress, and her lips were a soft pink as they smiled at him.

'I found her,' he said. 'I found her on the beach a few days ago, can't remember now. Thought she was dead. Found her lying in the water on the beach at low tide, face down in the water, soaked through. Soaked in that black dress she wears. Lifted her out and got her onto the sand like the lifeguards do, pumped her chest. After a bit some water came out of her mouth and then she spat a whole lot more out and she sat up and then she just looked at me like she does and she smiled, and she's been here since.'

'You found her on the beach?'

'Few days ago.'

'And she was lying in the water dressed like she is now?'

'And soaking wet. And once she'd sat up, she was up and running about the beach and then her clothes were all dry and she had me dancing on the sand.'

'You danced with her?'

'Yes. Strange. There she was, smiling away and dancing round and round on the sand, and then she waves me over and I see she wants me to dance too, and there I am, old Sam, dancing about on the beach. Never forget that.'

'But Sam, she must be someone's child, surely people must be looking for her?'

'I took her into the village, walked around with her, no-one wanted her. Nothing in the newspapers. Was going to ask again, take her to the village again and ask, but we didn't. Didn't seem to matter.'

'But did you go to the police?'

'Why? She done nothing wrong. Why bother the police, they got a job to do. They busy, like everyone, why make a fuss? I don't mind, if she wants to stay here. I stay here. Why can't she, if she wants?'

The little girl was on the floor, playing with the black cat. Isobel looked down at her. It was a mad story, but everything about it she knew was true. She knew there was no missing girl in the village, and she knew that Sam had no relatives – Marion or Michael would have mentioned it last night. She knew that Sam was telling the truth. It was an extraordinary story, but it was true.

'Where do you think she's come from?'

Sam thought about this question. Isobel was right, the girl must have come from somewhere. But as soon as he had seen her lying on the beach, he had known that her arrival did not accord with his understanding of the beach and its place in the world. People just didn't turn up on the beach; animals did, pieces of wrecked ships did, but not people.

But all that meant was that he didn't understand it, and that was no great surprise, because if you lived here and spent every day here and went down to the beach every day, you realised just how much you didn't understand. There were many things he would never understand, and it was like the way he tried to listen to the surf and hear just one part of its noise – he couldn't even do that and he'd lived all his life here. He could talk all day about the things he didn't understand, and the girl turning up on the beach would just be one of a long, long list. Was it any wonder he had not thought further about it?

'Where she from? You ask this question, you ask that. Questions all day. What is it? Is it like school: you answer the questions or you can't go home?'

Isobel could see that he was not annoyed. He was looking at her and discussing the issue calmly.

'She wants to stay here? Fine. She causes no bother, she helps around the house, she likes it here I think. Since mother died I've had no-one else here, there's mother's bed there she can use. She doesn't want to talk? Fine. No rules here about talking or not talking. She's welcome to stay if that's what she wants.'

'Do you think it is what she wants?'

'She's here, isn't she? What about you? You know what you want? You're here aren't you, you said you wanted to see mother's house. You must want to be here. She's the same as me, she's the same as you.'

Isobel thought, I wish she was. I wish I was her.

Instead, she said, 'Well, it's a remarkable story. What a pity your mother couldn't have met her. I know she would have felt the same way as you.'

'Do you think so? Was she happy, mother? Do you remember her being happy?'

'Oh yes. Yes, I think she was very happy here.'

Sam nodded and smiled.

'Good. That's good. Sometimes now I don't remember her so well. It's good you remember that.'

Isobel felt a sudden need to go, to be back on her own. 'I should go. You've been so kind. I should go now.'

The girl sat back up in her chair and looked at her.

'It was nice of you to have me and to make such a lovely tea. Thank you. It's been so nice. I must go now.'

Isobel picked up her bag, and smiled at them as they stayed seated at the table. She ducked back out of the open front door and across the concrete yard and out to the path, and she almost ran down the path, not looking back.

That evening, Sam and the girl ate a supper of runner beans and potatoes from the garden, and lamb chops from the farmer's freezer with gravy. Sam fried the chops in butter, and the girl cut up the runner beans which she had collected in a wicker basket from the garden at the back. Sam showed her how he liked to squash the boiled potatoes into the buttery juice from the chops. She watched him with interest as he mashed the potato with his fork, then she did the same.

At the end of the meal, as it was still light, she took the plates out and scraped the last pieces of potato onto the wall, and waited while the seagulls flew down to pick it up.

'I forgot to ask her if she would help us choose you some new clothes.'

The girl turned to look at him, then back at the seagulls.

'I've had a look in mother's cupboard and there's a couple of old pairs of trousers might fit you, and a couple of shirts, but you should have a few things of your own. Swimming costume, nice frock, hat. I thought we could get Isobel to help us choose you some – old Sam wouldn't know. Need a woman for that.'

The girl turned around again, frowned at Sam, then ran into the front room where her bed was and carefully picked up the pink rubber shoes which she kept on her pillow, the price tag still clipped to one of the straps. She bought them back out into the yard and showed them to Sam, glaring at him. He laughed.

'Oh I know you like them, I seen the way you look

at them. You mean I can choose you some clothes the same way? Well I don't know, I think clothes for a little girl is different. I just wouldn't know. I wouldn't feel right choosing you a dress – what if I chose you one that wasn't right and I didn't know and you didn't look right?'

He remembered when he was a little boy how his mother would occasionally take him into the village to buy a new jacket or a pair of shorts, and he could remember even now the seriousness of those occasions, the significance of each of the many elements of the purchase: the drama of the handing over of the money, the worried look on his mother's face as he stood in front of the mirror in the little clothes shop trying on a jacket, the long walk back home with the item wrapped up in brown paper clutched under his arm. What a complicated, complex activity! He had merely chanced his arm with the pink shoes, he wouldn't like to risk it a second time.

'No, it needs a woman's skill,' he said seriously to her. 'She said she was staying in the village, we could call on her, ask her to help next time we go in. She'd be pleased to help, she seems friendly enough.'

The girl sniffed and returned her shoes to their pride of place on her pillow, and Sam went back into the kitchen to clear their dishes.

How strange that his life was now suddenly, how would he put it, womanised? Before the girl's arrival he wouldn't have said that his life had a particularly male or female flavour. His acceptance of his place in the life about him did not involve an awareness of his sex or even character – it was more of a flow of things and animals and time and weather, all linked together like a sea.

Yet he knew the world depended on it: the mating of the seabirds in the spring, the transmission of seed from one plant into another, the eggs that spilled out of the guts of the mackerel when he ripped their stomachs open with his knife. His own abstinence from sex, largely self-imposed through his isolation from other people after his mother died, did not unduly concern him. His occasional experiences of sex during his times away on construction sites were hardly satisfactory: usually alcohol-fuelled, late night couplings, sometimes paid for, sometimes not.

At the time the desire that raged through his huge body seemed overwhelming, and he would often repeat the pattern which became familiar to him of trawling bars in the rough areas of the towns where he was working until he found a woman willing to satisfy his urge, and they would kiss drunkenly in alleyways or occasionally hotel rooms and he would surrender himself. But the aftermath was never joyful, unlike the shout of triumph at climax, and he would feel stale and unsettled, and would leave as soon as he could.

Perhaps it was the association with alcohol which meant he did not notice the disappearance of sex from his own life, because since his return to live with his mother he found he did not need to drink in the evenings as he often had done when he was away. Soon after his return home he stopped buying the few cans of beer from the village grocery, and the quiet pattern of his life developed.

Could it have been different? Could one of those briefly-known women have made some connection with him, could he have found a partner as his father did? It was unlikely. There was little about his years working away from the village which felt true to him, and the occasional noisy bouts of drinking and the blurred couplings were all a part of the crude and physical life on the construction sites.

He never knew how his mother and father met, but he idealised their short marriage, and saw in it a perfect story of human companionship and stoicism which he felt humbled him. How was he to measure up to a father who had given his life so selflessly, to a mother who had battened down her grief and had raised him so perfectly and yet with such struggles? He, old Sam, whose only contribution had been to work and fight and brawl on building sites, and lie stupid with drink in the gutter after an argument with a whore – of course he could never achieve the grace of his parents' marriage.

And so poor Sam had drifted away from people and quietly lived amongst the elements of the world and forgot about love.

He turned from the sink, hearing the girl step back into the room. She was wearing one of his old nightgowns, carefully preserved by his mother from his childhood. She looked tired, but contented.

'Long day again, little one?' he said. 'You want some warm milk before you go to sleep?'

She smiled sleepily, and sat down at the kitchen table while Sam put milk on to heat on the stove.

'Turned old Sam's life upside down, that's for sure,' he said. He was still very aware that his conversations now were specifically addressed to the girl, as though she had emerged into his life with such a presence that the familiar objects of his conversations – the fridge, the cooker, the house – seemed to have melted back into the distance. As with the conversation earlier with Isobel, he was not sure about it, but he accepted it.

'What do you think, then? We make a good team you and me?'

She grinned at him.

'You know what's going on all right. You may not talk, and that's all right, but you understand old Sam, don't you? A good team, yes, I think so. A good team.'

He poured the hot milk from the saucepan into a mug and passed it to her, then sat down himself at the table.

'We'll have to sort some things out eventually. Suppose you'll need to go to school one day. Need to get some learning. You can go to Sam's old school, they're all right there, you won't mind them. I'll have tea ready for you when you come home.'

She sipped her milk, her little eyelids flickering with tiredness.

'All that to come. No hurry. First thing is, get you some clothes. I think that Isobel is the one for that job. I don't mind her. We'll go and see her soon I think.'

He took the empty mug from the child, and she got down and padded softly to bed. Sam washed her mug in the sink and set it to dry on the draining board. He went into the front room which was lit in a gentle, wavy light by the candles in the window, and bent over the bed and patted the little dark head which was nestled into the pillow, the pink shoes beside her.

'Good night little one,' he said. 'You sleep well.'

She was asleep already.

There was a patter of rain on the window pane, and a gust of wind blew against the glass. The weather that had been threatening all afternoon was finally here. He walked over to the door to his bedroom, which was open, and in the pale light from the candles in the front room he could see the cat curled up on his bed.

'Best place for you too,' he said quietly.

Before the rain really set in, he thought he would check outside to make sure he and the girl had not left anything out. He took a torch from on top of the fridge and went out into the yard. The wind was blowing hard now, and the rain glistened on his face. Soon it would be pouring down. It was very dark, the clouds now covering the whole sky and obscuring the moon and the stars.

Sam walked to the edge of the yard at the back, and along the rear of the house where he could see the newly varnished cladding. He took three steps up into the garden where the girl had picked runner beans earlier. Up here in the vegetable garden he was raised up so that he could see over the flat roof of the house, and in the rain-specked dark he could see glimpses of the crests of waves down in the bay below, and in between the rush of the wind he could hear the surf crash on the shore.

He did not like these nights so much, where the wind was high and the waves were cresting and the rain was biting harder and harder. He did not like the wild inter-mingling of sounds, the chaotic drama of noise and the huge pressure of the wind and the piercing of the rain. Standing now in the vegetable garden, his torch down at his side glowing on a circle of earth, he thought of his father clutching to the bow of the lifeboat as it smashed through the waves, and not for the first time he felt he could hear cries in the dark, cries of fear amongst the howl of the wind and the beating of the surf.

It was a bad night.

He turned away once more, and went back to the house and into the warm, light kitchen and shut and bolted the door behind him.

And while Sam cleared up the final things in the kitchen, Isobel still sat beneath the lighthouse, her legs dangling over the edge of the low wall facing the sea, the wind throwing biting tears of rain into her face.

She had walked from Sam's house to the point of the headland, and had stood for a moment by a gate which led off the coast path. Beyond the gate a small concrete yard and a low building, then the lighthouse itself, tall and white against the sky. There was nobody around, the lighthouse was automated now.

She undid the latch of the gate and walked into the yard. The lighthouse stood on the rocky end of the headland, and she walked around it until she had it to her back and there was just a drop of rock between her and the sea about fifty or sixty feet below. She crouched down, sat on the rocky ledge so that all she could see was the solid mass of the sea extending out south from the headland as far as the horizon.

She sat at the edge of the land as the sky reddened over to the west and the waves crested below her and the rain stung her face. A few hundred yards away, Sam tucked the girl's blanket up over her shoulder and said 'Goodnight little one', although she was already asleep, and he walked out to the back of the house and up into the vegetable garden and looked out over the flat roof at the turbulent sea.

And the wind gusted over the headland and the waves crashed onto the beach and a last flock of cormorants flew low over the churning sea.

Ten

Just before midday, Isobel sat in front of the village registrar and waited while he signed her mother's death certificate. She sniffed once or twice – it had been a cold and wet walk home last night.

'There is a small registration charge,' the man said, without looking up. 'You can pay at the desk on the way out.'

He finished writing, dried the ink with a blotter, and slid the certificate into a brown envelope. He passed it to Isobel.

'My condolences once more,' he said, and smiled briefly.

'Yes,' said Isobel.

Back at the cottage she put the envelope down on the coffee table, and went into the kitchen to make some tea.

'Well, that's it, mummy,' she said out loud. 'I've brought you home. What shall we do, put you on the mantlepiece with my postcards?'

She took her tea into the dining room where her work was laid out. She thought: I would like to be able to write to someone too. Like Héloise. I would like to be able to write to someone, and to get a reply. Something to tell me how to move on. How to live now. Because it seemed as though she had reached an ending, and she was unsure now of where to go next.

Who would she write to?

She sat down at the table. She shivered, although the bad weather of the night before had passed already and the house was not cold. She drank her tea, and sat still, hearing only the ticking of the clock on the dining room mantlepiece.

Isobel sat at the table all afternoon, not picking up any of the books or papers in front of her, not stirring to make a drink or something to eat. She sat still, her breath shifting the air silently in the dark little room, her hands flat on the surface of the table, as the afternoon light crept by the window.

'You need an early night tonight, you do.'

Sam was looking at the girl who was scraping the last juice of the beef stew from her plate with a wedge of bread. Her black hair hung over her face, but Sam had seen her eyes and they were tired.

'You were busy again today. Should go to bed before it's dark. Another long day today.'

They had spent the day on the farm, and in between helping Sam by passing him bricks for the wall he was building, she had played happily with the cats and the chickens in the yard. The farmer was out in the fields all day preparing for harvest, and they did not see anyone all the time they were there.

At one point Sam had paused in his work and had watched the girl as she played with some of the chickens, and he chuckled again to see her pretend to be one of them, imitating their jerky little runs and bobbing her head up and down.

She was happy in her surroundings always, there had not once been any sense of concern or fear or discontent. It was as though she had grown up with him and had absorbed his own contented sense of belonging in the world about them. If there was no job for her to do or he was busy at something, she would easily begin her own game, or start a new task, or go about with whatever animals were there.

Earlier in the day, before they left for the farm and while Sam was making up sandwiches for their lunch, he had seen her clamber up onto the white wall at the edge of the yard and stand on tip-toe with her arms outstretched as the seagulls flapped and squawked over her, and it was as though she was joining in their discussions and was a part of them, her little outstretched fingers straining to reach up to the birds swooping about her. And the gulls, too, seemed to accept her presence, and he almost imagined her leaping up and gliding herself amongst them in the sky.

'Come on, give me that plate and you go and get yourself ready for bed. I'm going to go down on the beach later, when you're asleep, and cast out for some bass off the beach. The water's been running strong in these winds today, will have pushed some bass into shore. Old Sam'll get us a couple of nice bass for lunch tomorrow.'

She looked at him and her little face broke into a big yawn and she rubbed her eyes and gave a little smile.

'And tomorrow we'll walk into the village and go and find that Isobel. Get her to help you find some clothes.'

The girl went off into the front room, and when Sam had finished clearing the dishes and washing them, leaving them to dry on the draining board, he went in to see her. Although daylight was still showing through the window, suffused with the red of the sunset to come, she was already asleep in the bed.

He tucked the blanket up over her shoulder, then closed the curtains, and said softly, 'Off for a bit of fishing now. Not long. You sleep well, be back soon.'

Outside in the yard he opened one of the storage sheds and pulled out a fishing rod. He stood for a moment by the wall and looked out over the bay. The wind was dying down now, but the sky was still thick with cloud, and over the western headland it was streaked with red and orange as the sun began to drop. The beach down below was empty, and he looked forward to standing down there in the wet sand and casting out.

Once he was down on the beach he walked to within about ten or fifteen feet of the water's edge, and set the handle of the rod down on the sand so that the tip of it stood straight above his head. He found where the lure, a silvery metal fish, was hooked onto one of the eyes that held the line, and he carefully prized the hook off the eye and let the lure dangle loose in the breeze. He lifted the rod up and checked over the reel, tugging the line with the switch to 'off' to make sure it caught cleanly, and then opening the switch and pulling a little line through to make sure the spindle did not rub.

He looked up and scanned the sea in front of him, dark and strong and smelling very freshly in the evening light of salt, and he decided where he would cast his line. Don't want to let the current take the lure down onto the rocks on the left there, he thought. But the bass will be heading for the rocks all the same, that's where they'll find their supper. Want to run across them as they head in to the rocks, divert their attention. He looked behind him and saw that the beach was empty, then he leant the rod back behind his head so that the lure hung down almost to touch the sand, and he pushed the switch on the reel open with his thumb and dipping his right shoulder he leant back, then with a clean rush he swung the rod back over him and held it out in front of him, the tip pointing up above the horizon. At the same time he let his thumb free of the switch and the line shot out of the reel as the weight of the lure pulled it fast behind it and it soared through the evening sky and landed in the water forty or fifty yards out to sea.

He waited for a second or two for the lure to fall down into the weight of the water, and just before he sensed it was going to reach the seabed, he began to reel in. The line tugged the lure back towards him, jerking through the dark water, the silvery metal spinning and the hook wriggling off the back. It took about thirty seconds to reel the lure in, and Sam soon settled into the rhythm of casting, waiting, reeling in, lifting up the tip of the rod and leaning back and casting once more.

He loved everything about this: the calm rhythm, the splash of the lure into the water, the feel of the wet sand under his shoes, the evening breeze on his face, the gentle noise of the surf, the occasional call of a gull, the emptiness of the beach. Gradually the light faded into grey, and he looked over at the smear of orange on the western headland until finally it was gone and the beach was dark with the cloudy night. No stars tonight. But he could still see the water stretch out in front of him and his line taut and jumpy as he reeled it in.

After quarter of an hour he felt a strike, a jolt on the line just after he had begun to reel in, and he spoke to the rod as he reeled faster:

'That's it, do your work, keep a hold of him for me. Not sure what you've got, mind. Not sure. But bring him in, don't let go of him, that's a good job, keep going.'

And as the line shortened more and more, he saw a splash in the shallows and he waded into the water holding the rod high above his head and passed his

134

hand down the wet line and pulled the fish up out of the water.

'Thought so. Dog fish. No good.'

The fish, long and thin like an eel, wrapped itself around his arm as he held its head to pull out the hook from inside its mouth.

'All muscle you are,' he said as the dog fish clung to his arm. 'No good for us, no good at all.'

Finally he dislodged the hook from the throat of the fish and he swung it back out into the water.

'You'll be all right,' he called out into the dark. 'Bit of a shock, but you'll be all right. Just keep off my lure.'

He fell back into the rhythm of his fishing.

Another ten minutes passed, and then he felt another strike, and this time the strike was strong, vital, like a shock. He felt the tremor from the line shoot up his arm, and his heart beat strongly.

'Come on now,' he said.

He pulled back on the rod, reeled in, let the rod down again, gave it more play. He could feel the strength of the fish at the end of the line.

'Nice,' he said into the dark. 'Don't go losing him, mind.'

Slowly, he reeled more and more of the line in. The tip of the rod was vibrating now, and he could feel the tension sing in the line.

Finally there was a splash ahead of him. He waded back into the water and lifted the catch out. A bass, not a bad size, three, maybe four pounds. It flapped on the end of the line and he could see the run of silver scales down its sides.

He tucked the rod under his arm and held the fish by the gills and removed the hook, which had just lodged in its lip. Then he held its head with his left hand and yanked it back quickly, and heard a click as its neck snapped.

'Oh!'

It was a woman's voice, startled. Sam turned round.

'Who's there?'

The beach was too dark for him to see very far.

'It's...' The woman's voice in the dark was hesitant. 'It's Isobel. I'm sorry, I didn't mean to disturb you.'

With the rod still tucked under his arm and the bass hanging limp off his right hand, Sam felt in his jacket pocket with his free hand for his torch. He pulled it out, switched it on, and played the beam back behind him onto the beach. About twenty yards away to his left the beam caught Isobel's face, quite white in the beam of the torch and she looked straight back at him.

For a second, another of those tiny precious moments, Isobel sensed in the chill darkness a connection, a thought that existed at each end of the beam of light.

The first thought was: what is she doing here? She knew that was Sam's reaction, she could tell that without needing to see his face, which was just a dark shape to her at this moment behind the glare of his torch. And she had been thinking that thought too, had been thinking it for hours as she paced about the beach in the dying light.

She hadn't really made any decision earlier in the cottage: at six o'clock she had suddenly pushed all her papers off the dining table, ran upstairs to put on warm clothes and had headed off once more for the coastal path. Perhaps amongst her jagged thoughts that day, the idea of going to the beach, to watch over Sam's house, had formed itself in her mind, and she had allowed it to form without being aware of it until by the end of the afternoon she simply knew that was what she was going to do.

As she passed by the lighthouse, halfway along the walk to the great bay, she paused to look out over the end of the land at the stony grey sea and she wondered aloud then, what am I doing here? And aloud she had answered herself, I don't know. She was agitated, but beneath the flurry of her thoughts, which were random, unspecific, she sensed a calmness which was soothing. She was aware of this, lying in the background of her mind: a certainty.

On the beach when she got there it was still light, and she walked about looking at the stones and shells on the sand and that quiet clarity below her conscious confusion remained, so that even as she muttered aloud to herself, 'What the hell am I doing here?' she was not unhappy. In fact she enjoyed sensing the presence of this unknowable certainty somewhere inside her and wondering at it. She was on her own, and there was no-one to witness her odd behaviour, and she was happy to be here on the beach as the sun slid down behind the clouds and this idea, whatever it was, glowed inside her like an ember.

And then suddenly she had seen Sam appear at the top of the steps from his house. She had retreated into the gloom under one of the overhanging cliff rocks at the edge of the beach and watched him as he walked down the steps slowly and calmly, a fishing rod in his right hand, an old waxed jacket over his shoulders and beach shoes with no socks which sank a little into the damp sand as he walked across the beach in front of her down by the water's edge.

She watched transfixed as his measured, deliberate steps seemed to freeze in time with each pace, just at the moment when his back foot would be about to lift up from the sand, and she felt as though each time she were almost waiting to see if the foot would leave the sand. She would never forget that, the moment when his whole body seemed caught as in a film, in a frame, and then it moved on and then a second later, again, there was a moment caught in time. She was so overwhelmed by this observation that she kept holding her breath and then letting it out again after a while, her pulse racing.

'What are you doing here?' asked Sam.

His voice sounded almost conversational, and the thick cloud overhead and the background crush of the surf dampened any echo. He thought: again, this is out of the run of things for the beach. But he also knew that he had changed over the last week, and her presence did not cause him immediately to look away. He could recall first seeing her on the bench last week on the cliff path and his eyes looking past diagonally as he had learned to do over the years, but now he had no sense of alarm, no reluctance to engage. Was this what the girl had done?

Yes, Isobel thought. I know that is what he is thinking. All she could see was his huge shape, dark behind the beam, and the outline almost in shadow of the dead fish hanging off his right hand. But there is more. It is not just that he wonders why I am here – he also wonders how I have let myself be here.

Because that is the other part of this moment – we both know that everything has changed. Look now: he has just killed. The fish is hanging off him. I came here on my own. I am without anything, and he has everything now.

'I… I'm not sure.'

'Are you cold? Your voice sounds like you're cold. Have you been out here long? It's cold on this beach after sunset, you should remember that.'

'I'm all right. I'm sorry I disturbed you. I'm not cold.'

'You sound cold.'

Oh God, she thought, there is no escape. She was completely cold, she realised he was right. She hadn't noticed. Over the last hour she had stood rigid watching the movements of his huge limbs and she hadn't noticed the damp evening cold creep through her clothes. It was the second night running that she had been out, and now she felt it.

She's not right, Sam thought. She doesn't sound right at all. He began to walk through the shallows of the water towards her, the bright yellow light of the torch still on her face.

'You'd better have my coat,' he said as he drew closer.

'No, no, really, I'm fine… I just… I…'

She could see the beam coming closer and closer, and it suddenly looked like the sun, as though with every second she was being drawn closer and closer to the sun. What was the story about that? About Icarus and his wings and flying closer and closer to the sun? With every second now she could feel the heat and the power of the sun and she struggled to remember the story. Then another image of the fish with its neck breaking, only now it was in slow motion and she could hear the noise of the tearing bone louder and louder.

Sam saw her begin to fall, and he dropped the rod and the fish and leaped forwards and was just in time to catch her back as she collapsed onto the sand.

'Fainted,' he said. 'She's fainted.'

He lay her on the sand and played the beam of the torch over her face, which was completely white. He stepped back to pick up the rod and the fish which lay on the sand behind him, and then he brought them back and put them beside her.

'Not used to the nights. Too long away I suppose,' he said. 'Gets cold down here at night.'

He knew that there was still the unanswered question in the air of what she was doing here, but he also knew that in some way the answer lay with him. And again, he realised how, as she lay silent on the cold sand, he was not threatened. He did not feel that the balance of his life was challenged. He felt strong.

'Better get you back to the warm.'

He crouched down and put both huge arms under her, and he lifted her up so her head was supported by his left arm. Then, still holding her, he leant down on his knees over the sand so that his right hand could feel for the rod. His fingers found it, then they found the fish, and he tucked one of his fingers into the gills of the fish and then he stood up slowly. Isobel's unconscious body was draped over his two massive arms and underneath her the rod and the fish dangled from his fingers. In his left hand below her head he still had the torch, and he set off back along the beach.

'City people,' he said to the dark beach as they walked. 'City people, forget about how to look after themselves. Rushing about, forget what they know. Come down here not prepared, didn't she? Not prepared.'

He would get her home, get her into the warm. Make some tea. She would be all right.

He trudged slowly along the dark beach, with the noise of the surf to his right and the sky black with cloud. After a few minutes Isobel began to come out of her faint. The heat and the light of the sun had gone and as her consciousness re-appeared inside her like a dawn she felt herself being carried.

She knew he was carrying her. She stayed silent and wondered at the feeling of allowing every muscle in her body to be relaxed as she contoured into his arms and his chest. She could smell the scent of him everywhere like hay dampened by a summer rainfall, and she understood finally that there was a certainty and at last she was inside it. She kept her eyes closed and he carried her home.

Eleven

I sobel lay on Sam's bed, listening to the quiet sounds of preparation from the kitchen.

He had carried her through the kitchen and then through a darkened front room which was just illuminated by a small candle in a glass in the window. She had briefly looked through half closed eyes and had seen the little bed in the corner of the room where the girl lay tucked up and fast asleep, her dark hair messy over the pillow, and oddly a pair of bright pink rubber shoes beside her head. He had carried her across this room, past dark old furniture, and through a door at the other end into a small bedroom. She had let herself be lain down upon the single bed which was in one corner, and then Sam had lit a gas light on the opposite wall, which hissed out a yellow light into the bare room.

Now she lay here listening to the sounds from the kitchen, and she lifted herself up so that she could look around the room. It was bare and empty like a cell, with just a wardrobe at the end and a wooden chair in the other corner with an old sweater draped over its arms. There was nothing on the walls, and the curtains which he had drawn after lighting the gas lamp were paisley-patterned synthetic. The bed she was lying on was longer than usual, and was covered in a blue eiderdown which had been neatly made that day.

The certainty inside her of which she had become more and more aware through the evening as she paced around the beach flooded through her now, and she had no fear. She felt like she was bathing in a beautiful calm.

Was this what this certainty was about? The sense that she did not have to retain control, that she could let her mind relax its grip just as she let her muscles untense into Sam's great, fragrant body? Yes, because for Isobel absolute certainty was like a state of grace. Faced with an infinite number of actions and outcomes, the one that was taken without a second thought was never regretted. Without consciously realising it, this was how her whole life had been. But now she recognised it, now she finally understood it, she could see that it was this certainty which Héloise experienced when she submitted to a life behind nunnery walls, a banishment which ultimately offered her complete joy.

Isobel had always appeared wilful, capricious to others; never respectful of convention, quixotic in her decisions. Yet each time she took a new path, she knew how simple it would been to have made a different choice; how arbitrary that choice really was. When she talked to people, they never seemed to doubt that their favourite colour was green or that they loved their children, when all

Isobel could ever imagine was a host of alternatives, like a flickering canopy of stars.

Now here she was, lying on a strange man's bed in the stuttering gas light, and she was utterly and joyfully happy because she knew that there was nowhere else she could be.

Sam talked quietly to the cooker as it heated the water in the kettle. He did not want the girl to wake up, although he knew she slept soundly, but he also did not want to disturb Isobel, whom he presumed still to be in a faint as she lay quiet on his bed.

'Well, this is another thing, isn't it?' he murmured in his soft, deep voice. 'First one female, then another, both on the beach, both not supposed to be there. That's another thing, isn't it?'

He wandered over to the sink and looked out through the window, where all was still black. The cloudy sky and the light from inside the kitchen made it impossible to make out anything of the sea, but there was the regular flash of the lighthouse over to the left, and the mast light of what must have been a trawler heading out south west.

'This is a strange night,' he said, to the room generally.

Yet although the recent events presented a disturbance to his routine, still he did not feel perturbed by the changes, and this he noticed and was surprised by. He had become so used to his immersion into the world around him, so accustomed to yielding to the flow of the seasons and the tides and the weather and the everyday physical requirements of his day, that he had not specifically noticed the absence up until the last week of human beings.

Perhaps he had grown so used to walking past them, his eyes fixed on the distance, that he had really forgotten about them. And now suddenly two had appeared together in his life, and in their own ways had merged into his life without friction: the girl through her natural ease and obvious pleasure which she took from being with him, and Isobel from the extraordinary connection which she brought with her to his mother.

In fact, by providing him with images which he could never have possessed himself, she had almost closed a circle which had been left open by the unexpected death of his mother ten years ago. As though having someone else now who could validate his own memories and reinforce them with more could provide some kind of finality, some resolution.

'I won't question it,' he said. 'There's something here and it's not for me to question it, not old Sam. That's not for Sam. Keep busy, go quietly, that's for Sam.'

The steam hissed from the mouth of the kettle, and he went back to the cooker and turned off the gas. All he could think of was to try to revive Isobel with a mug of hot, sweet tea – he had not had to deal with anyone fainting on the beach from cold before.

'City people,' he chuckled deeply. 'Know everything, know nothing. Got too cold out there. Ah well. Wake her quietly, give her some tea, then we'll see.'

He took the mug of tea through the darkened front room and into his bedroom, where Isobel was lying on the bed, her eyes closed. He sat down on the edge of the bed, and his great size blocked the light from the gas lamp and cast her face into shade.

Isobel, her eyes closed, felt the weight of him as he sat on the edge of the mattress. She dared not open her eyes. Now it was beyond choice, and she felt simply the rush of blood through her body.

'Isobel.'

His voice was very soft, and very deep.

'Isobel. Can you hear me?'

He placed the back of two thick fingers against her forehead.

'Are you able to hear me? You're cold still, you need to drink this, revive you.'

She felt the gentle pressure of his fingers on her forehead and did not want to disturb this moment.

'I don't know anything else,' he said. 'Hot tea, that's best for you I think.'

Now she would look at him, and she opened her eyes and saw his huge shape sitting on the edge of the bed. This strong, huge man.

'There,' he said. 'I knew you could do it.'

He passed the mug towards her.

'Don't talk now, drink some of this tea, get the warmth back in you.'

She sat on one elbow and took the mug from him wordlessly. Now everything was moving slowly, and she sipped the hot tea for what seemed like an age, then passed it back to him.

'You've only had a couple of tiny sips, need more,' he said, gently pressing a finger to the mug.

She put it back to her lips, and drank, and again this all seemed to be lasting forever.

'Better,' he said, and took the mug back and set it down on the floor.

'Thank you,' she said, her voice very quiet.

The gas lamp hissed from the wall. Neither of them said anything.

How strange, she thought. That it should be here, in this odd little house, in this cell-like room. After everything, after all her life, after all of it, that it should be here.

She smiled.

'I've made a bit of a fool of myself, haven't I?'

Isobel spoke softly, looking up at Sam's eyes.

'I don't know. It happens.'

'Does it?'

They were quiet again. Isobel could hear only the roar of her blood. Sam looked down at her thin fleece, then back to her face.

'What were you doing there?'

'Watching you.'

'Watching me?'

'Yes.'

'Why were you watching me?'

'I don't know.'

Sam shifted his foot slightly, and nudged the mug on the floor, which scraped on the cold stone. From the other room came a sound of sleep from the girl, a sigh of sleep as she turned in her blankets.

They looked at each other.

'Sam?'

He looked at her with his rough, strong face and his blue eyes and the sand grey stubble around his chin.

'Sam, I don't want to go home.'

'That's all right.'

'Is it?'

'Yes, it's all right.'

'I mean… if you want me to, I will. But I don't want to.'

Sam looked at her lying on his bed. This beautiful, pale woman with her blonde hair messy on the pillow.

'I'll leave you now,' he said. 'Some sleep, that's what you need. I'll leave you now.'

He could sleep out on the bench with a blanket. There would be no more rain, the wind was blowing west. He often chose to sleep outside, listening to the surf as he fell asleep.

He stood up and reached his hand out for the handle of the bedroom door.

'No!'

She let this out weakly, involuntarily.

'What's wrong?'

He came back and stood over the bed. She put out her hand and touched his and felt how rough his skin was, like sail cloth that had dried in the wind and the sun.

'Nothing,' she whispered. 'Would you just talk to me for a bit? Tell me things.'

He stood there, and her hand felt tiny and soft and delicate to him, and he slowly turned his wrist while her fingers stroked his skin.

'What things?'

'Anything. About your fishing. Your house. Anything.'

'Will it help you sleep, do you think?'

He felt still her fingers on his skin, and he was confused now. Why did she want him to talk? There was nothing to say. He felt also a feeling that was unusual, a feeling that stemmed from the touch of her finger on his hand.

'About anything?'

'Yes,' she whispered.

She pulled now on his hand, and he found himself sitting down on the edge of the long bed.

'Don't go. Please don't go. Please. Just talk to me for a bit.'

And his deep voice began to talk about the house, and

how his great grandfather had built it, and how his father and his grandfather had built the steps down onto the beach, and how his mother had given him this bedroom. He spoke of the work that needed to be done constantly to resist the battering of the sea-filled winds, how he had to rub down the wood of the windows every other year and re-coat them, and how he had to chip off the paint from the outside wall sometimes to let it dry out fully over the summer before applying a new white protective coat.

After all these years, to be sitting here, talking to a woman in his bedroom. This was so strange, this was unaccountable. But it was like those rip tides, when you don't fight them, but you relax and flow with the current, out into the sea and way away to another part of the shore where it is safe. He felt himself drifting far out, far out from the shore.

Slowly she pulled at his hand now, and his face came down lower, so that he was just inches away from her now. He stopped talking and looked at her.

'I don't want you to go Sam,' she said. 'You won't ever go, will you?'

Sam heard her voice, and he heard also the sound of the surf from the window, and the wind in the air outside.

'You could shut the door now, and stay here with me,' she whispered.

Sam could smell a soft sweetness from her hair, he

could see her eyes wide in the dark.

'Shut the door, you say?'

'Yes.'

He was silent for a second, then he heaved back off the bed and reached out to the bedroom door and gently pushed it shut. He came back to the bed.

Isobel reached for his hand with hers, and slowly pulled as she felt the pounding of the blood inside her and she lay on her side and pulled him down beside her. Sam could hear the surf loudly now, as though he was back on the beach.

He lay beside her, their bodies touching and their faces suddenly so close to each other on the bed that they could smell the heat of each other's breath. She closed her eyes as their lips touched and he thought how beautifully soft her lips were, and as they kissed he brought his hand up and brushed the blonde hair from her pale brow.

She opened her eyes so that she would see him.

'Is this right?' he said and she felt the warm sweet breath of the words on her face.

'Yes.'

She knew it must be and she felt with her fingers for the edge of his shirt and slipped her hand under to touch the skin of his back and to run her fingers slowly up the solid mass of Sam's body until she reached his neck. She clutched at his hair. She thought she could feel heat of the sun once more which was starting to melt her as his hand came down to her jeans and she took his hand in hers and guided it to the buttons at her waist.

'It's right,' she whispered, and then she said 'Oh!' as his hand felt down her legs, and soon she unfastened the jeans and eased them from her waist. He felt the hot damp hair between her legs and now he closed his eyes. Her tongue found his ear and still clutching his hair she reared up and he tugged at her jeans until they were off. She climbed onto him and looking at him now and smiling she pulled off her fleece and her T-shirt and her bra and then she reached down and undid the buttons of Sam's shirt and she kissed his chest which was wiry with hair.

Sam could hear the waves now, the noise of the surf, crashing loudly in his head as he looked up at her pale slim body above him. He felt her undoing the buckle of his belt and he helped her push his trousers down his legs and then she sat wet upon him and he held her hips and watched her smiling at him as she leant down over him.

He kissed her breasts and she let out a sigh and guided him inside her and then she sat back on him and said 'oh Sam, oh Sam!' and he stretched his fingers up to her mouth and she took his hand and pressed it against her face. He pushed inside her and they rocked together and she bit the flesh of his great fingers until he felt the tip of him burning and he let go with a low, deep groan.

She closed her eyes and the heat and the light of the sun flooded through her and engulfed her.

Twelve

In the morning when the girl awoke it was soon after dawn. The front room where she slept was grey with the new light, and for a few minutes she lay in the small bed with her eyes open. Outside the window a few starlings chattered, and the call of seagulls came too over the sound of the surf. At the end of her bed the cat lay curled asleep on the blanket. The door to Sam's room on the other side was shut.

Quietly the girl got up and dressed. Her black cotton dress was creased and she smoothed the fabric as she put it on. She was about to pick up Sam's old sandals when she paused, then reached over to her pillow and took the pink rubber shoes. She examined them carefully for a while, turning them over in her little hands, then she slipped her feet into them and closed the buckles.

She stood up and walked to the kitchen. The cat leaped softly from the bed and followed her, nudging her ankles, and she smiled at it. She took the bottle of milk out of the fridge and poured a little in a saucer and lay it down on the stone floor and watched as the cat licked it up. Then she rinsed the saucer in the sink and set it on the draining board with the previous evening's washing up. She looked around the kitchen, which was light now with the early morning, although the sun was not yet over the eastern headland. Then she opened the front door and the cat darted out in front of her and clambered over the wall at the back of the yard and disappeared into the heather and gorse of the cliff.

The girl walked around to the back of the house and began to climb down the steps which led to the beach. A seagull swooped over her and called out, and she looked up and waved. When she reached the sand she stood for a moment and looked down at her pink shoes, then she took two steps and looked back to see the imprint they left on the sand.

For the next hour the girl played on the beach and the sun appeared over the headland and shone down on her alone. Yesterday's clouds had finally cleared and the sky was bright blue. The girl climbed over the rocks looking into the pools which glittered in the morning light, then she ran down to the shore and stood at the edge of the water and looked out towards the horizon where a Navy frigate could be seen in the far distance steaming west.

A flock of oyster catchers, their bright orange beaks shining in the light against their black and white feathers, settled on the shore just behind the girl and they began to root about amongst the sand looking for early morning worms. She watched them, and occasionally she imitated their calls with a little high-pitched squeak which made her laugh, and her laugh carried across the silent bay.

She picked up flat stones from the sand, examining them in her hand before crouching low in front of the flat water and sending them skimming across the surface. This too made her laugh.

Then she turned her back on the sea and skipped past the birds along the sand, holding her arms out wide. She closed her eyes, and began to sway from side to side. Soon she was twirling around, her head back, and dancing on the beach in the fresh sunlight. It was as though there was a music playing across the whole of the bay, a music which had no sound, but which drove her on until, finally, she lay down on the sand.

The breeze played with the tips of her hair and the sun watched over her.

Eventually the girl made her way back to the steps and climbed back up to the house. She walked around the yard and into the kitchen, where Isobel was sitting at the kitchen table and Sam was pouring water from the kettle into the tea pot. He looked at her in the doorway.

'I saw you down on the beach,' he said. 'You up early.'

The girl looked at Isobel, who smiled at her.

'Hello,' said Isobel. 'Do you remember me?'

The girl sat at the table and put her hands on her lap and looked down. The room was quiet, then Sam coughed awkwardly and brought the tea pot over and set it down.

'Better have some breakfast, you up so early. Be hungry.'

He cut bread and placed it under the grill of the oven to toast.

Isobel continued to smile at the girl, then she looked at Sam.

'Sam, can I have toast too?'

Sam looked at her and grinned like a boy, and nodded.

'You must have been cold on the beach in that thin dress,' Isobel said to the girl.

She looked back at her without any expression in her little face. Isobel carried on smiling.

'I got so cold on the beach last night I fainted, and poor Sam had to bring me back here. I can't be as strong as you.'

Sam busied himself buttering and spreading toast with his back to them, then he brought two plates over and set them down in front of them. As he laid Isobel's plate in front of her, she placed her hand on his and looked up at him, and he blushed.

The girl ate her toast quickly and was finished by the time Sam returned to the table with a plate of his own. Isobel poured tea into the three cups in front of them and pushed one over the table to the girl.

'He looks after us, doesn't he?' she said to the girl.

The girl took the tea and looked at Sam, who was

munching toast, his eyes looking towards the middle distance.

'Do you know what I think?' continued Isobel. 'I think he's the last good man on earth. That's what I think. I think he's the last good man on earth.'

The room was silent once more apart from the crunching of the toast in Sam's mouth. The girl sipped her tea.

Isobel laughed.

'And you and I,' she said to the girl, 'you and I are the only people in the world who know it.'

This time the girl looked at her, and now her face was not expressionless, but had softened, and her eyes looked straight into Isobel's, and for a moment they held each other's gaze.

Sam coughed, and wiped a piece of crust from his chin.

'Was going to ask you a favour,' he said slowly to Isobel. 'We talked about it yesterday, me and the girl. About her clothes. She needs some clothes, some clothes for a little girl. Old Sam wouldn't know. We were going to come and see you today, ask if you could help us choose some for her.'

Isobel looked at Sam.

'You were going to come and see me?'

'For help. With her clothes.'

'Isn't that amazing?'

'Not really. You're the only woman we know.'

At this Isobel laughed out loud, and laughed so much the tears came to her eyes.

'I'm the only woman you know!' she said eventually.

Sam and the girl stared at her. She was still catching her breath from the laughter.

'Oh God, I can't tell you how much I like that. You really have no idea how much I like being the only woman you know.'

Sam smiled awkwardly.

'Could you help us?'

Isobel put her hand on his again.

'Of course,' she smiled, calm again. 'Of course. I'll take her into the village this morning and we'll buy some nice clothes. Won't we?'

She looked at the girl.

'I'll give you some money,' said Sam. 'I'm going to go up to the farm again this morning, put some more con-crete down. You don't need me there.'

'Don't be silly,' said Isobel. 'I'll buy them.'

There was silence again, and then Isobel stood up.

'Come on then, let's go and find you some pretty clothes,' she said to the girl brightly.

All three stood up and paused briefly in the bright morning sun of the kitchen. Sam shifted on his feet. The girl looked up at him, then Isobel took her hand and they both walked to the front door.

Isobel grasped the handle and pushed the door open, and the girl went out first, and Isobel followed and as she did so she turned her head and looked back at Sam as he stood motionless in the sunlit kitchen.

Isobel said, 'I love you Sam,' and was gone.

The hot, late summer sun beat down upon Sam as he scooped heavy spadefuls of coarse sand into the revolving mouth of the concrete mixer in the yard beside the farm. He was laying a path beside the stone wall which he had completed, and he was strong and enthusiastic as he plunged his spade into the pile of sand. He had taken his shirt off, and his sweat glistened in the sunlight and the muscles on his back bulged with each movement.

He felt truly invigorated. The events of the previous evening and night, shocking to him at first and the cause of embarrassment to him this morning at the breakfast table when he saw the girl, now filled him with joy.

Several times as he scooped sand and cement and hurled water from a bucket into the mix, he shouted out 'Ha!' to no-one and everyone, his big voice echoing in the empty yard. He had not seen the farmer or his wife, who must have been away in the fields, but if they had been there he felt as if he could have gone up to them with a broad smile and said, 'What a morning this is!'

'Oh, this is a new Sam!' he laughed out loud.

He had explained everything to the concrete mixer, how this beautiful, fragile city woman had entered into his life in such an extraordinary way. How she had brought with her memories of his mother that he would never otherwise have had, memories which were so precious and so accurate and so precise that they would be with him now for the rest of his life.

And then how this beautiful woman had given herself to him in a way he had never experienced and, again, had never imagined he would ever experience.

He did not feel that his life was different. For example, the concrete mixer which was churning the mix which he was spreading out between the timber stays – the mixer was as much a part of his life as all the other components with which he worked and to whom he talked. The *wholeness* of his life was not altered.

What had changed, first with the girl and now with Isobel, was that he had people in his life for the first time since his mother's death. He did not have to avert his eyes from them. He did not have to walk away from them. When he thought of how beautiful Isobel's pale white body looked to him as she sat upon him in the moonlit bedroom last night, he felt exultant.

For so many years now – perhaps in some ways all his life – Sam had not thought that human beings could have a place in his life. He had taught himself to pass by them quietly, to leave space between him and them.

Unlike a broken machine, which whatever it was Sam could eventually with his quiet patience fix, human beings with their complex malfunctionings could never be gently eased back into shape. They struck out, they clashed, they did the opposite of everything else in Sam's world: instead of forming a part of the whole so that they became invisible, they jarred against everything else so that they were all that could be seen.

So what was it that filled him with this euphoria this morning? Now, with these women in his life, why was he so thrilled?

He shook his head, grinning still, as he stood back to check the line of the path.

'Happy as a fool,' he said out loud, and he laughed. 'Happy as an old fool. Old Sam. Been on his own all these years. Not now. People to talk to quietly. Dancing on the beach.'

He laughed louder at that memory, and his laugh echoed about the yard.

'Dancing on the beach.'

He set back to work again, and threw more sand into the mixer. He continued to discuss this new perception of his life with the mixer as they both worked.

'Maybe,' he said, throwing handfuls of cement into the mix, 'maybe that's it: maybe old Sam was supposed to wait all this time.'

He thought about the disconcerting dreams and unsettled thoughts of his father which had plagued him recently. The strange imaginings seemed to him to lead nowhere. The anguished cries he thought he could hear from the men at sea – why? He paused for a moment in his work.

'Maybe no more of those dreams then?' he asked. 'Maybe some peace now? Maybe now the girl is here, now Isobel is here, maybe old father will be quiet now?'

Could that be true? Could his father somehow have been wanting him to be more settled? To be happy, as he had been in the short time he was given?

'It would be good if old father was quiet now,' said Sam. 'Don't like those dreams. Not right. Never dream about mother that way. Something that he's not happy with. Maybe he's quiet now.'

He scooped fresh concrete from the mixer and threw it in a slow, accurate way so that it landed heavily towards the end of the path he had almost completed.

He nodded as he returned for more.

'He wants me settled, women to look after me. Mother looked after him, now the girl and maybe Isobel too to look after Sam. Not on his own any more.'

He chuckled once more.

'Old Sam. With a family.'

There was no doubt, then, that Sam was happy. As he worked in the hot sun, sweating cleanly on his back. He gripped the shovel and swung it full of wet concrete onto the path.

So Sam, on this bright blue morning, wants to convince himself and the mixer that his nightmares will be over because he and Isobel had made love the night before. He thinks that the memory of his poor father will be at peace because now he has a family to look after him. He believes that the girl's silent companionship has signalled the end of his own quiet isolation.

Fine. Why not?

Only let this moment, as Sam hurls another clod of wet cement onto the path and it flies through the air, let this moment last forever, so that the oozing grey shape loses all momentum and Sam's big, strong, smiling face and his timbered arms and great bare sweating back and the churning mixer and the pile of fresh cement caught in mid-air all stay this way for minutes, hours, days, years.

And let his laugh ring out in the farmer's yard, echoing off the straight true line of the wall he has built, and dissolving into the great blue sky which stretches over the farmyard and across the fields and lanes and over the bay and the headland and the village and out to the horizon where the sky falls into the sea.

Thirteen

Maybe if she hadn't waited so long it would all have been different. Who knows? Maybe if on the way back into the village with the girl, Isobel hadn't thought about Abelard and Héloise and her book, maybe if she had just concentrated on what clothes she was going to buy. You know: it might have been different.

But Isobel had begun to think about her book, and as she followed the girl up the cut-through, following her pink shoes as they climbed the steep path, she realised that at last she could write her book. She was ready, and she would start the book with her own letter, written by her to Sam. At the start of the book, she would write to him, and this would be her introduction to her story, the story of her life, she supposed. Her letter, which she was composing already as they walked down the hill into the village, would, like Héloise's, seek advice and guidance. She would ask Sam how to live, and this excited Isobel: it finally made sense, it all finally made sense. And then the book would grow from there, and she would be able to write about all the things she had thought about all these years.

How extraordinary, to be able now to set the life that she had led within such a clear perspective.

She needed to set down the letter straight away, she felt sure that if she did not write it now, she might lose her thoughts. As they reached the village and they turned off left at the start of the promenade to reach the street where her mother's house was, Isobel suddenly thought of Marion. She could ask Marion to look after the girl for a couple of hours while she wrote the letter down, and then once she had done it they could go shopping. Sam had said he would be at the farm for a few hours, so there was no hurry. It wouldn't be fair on the girl to make her sit in her mother's gloomy little house in silence, she would enjoy playing with Marion's children. They should get to know each other anyway: they could all become friends soon.

'I'm going to introduce you to a nice lady, an old friend of mine,' she said to the girl as they walked towards the end of the row of cottages. 'I need to do something, and she has some lovely children you can play with. Then we'll go and buy your clothes, and we'll go back and show Sam. He'll be pleased, won't he?'

The girl looked at Isobel.

'I won't be long, and my friend is very nice.'

They reached the end of the street, and Isobel took the girl's hand as they crossed over. She rang Marion's doorbell.

'Hello,' said Isobel, when Marion answered. 'I've got a

surprise for you. This is Sam's child. I wondered whether you could look after her for a couple of hours? I'm taking her to buy some clothes, but I need to do a bit of work first in Mum's house. I shan't be long.'

'Isobel?' said Marion. 'What do you mean? What's happened?'

'Oh, I'll explain it all later. You won't believe it. Sam found her! In the sea!'

'Isobel.'

'We're going to look after her though, aren't we?' Isobel crouched down so her face was level with the girl. 'Me and Sam, we're going to look after you aren't we?'

And that was it. She didn't stay any longer, she just smiled as Marion tried to talk to her, and she didn't even really listen to what Marion was saying. Marion was calling out something even as Isobel crossed over the road and went into her mother's house, but Isobel just called back, 'I'll be back in a couple of hours, have fun!' and then she was in her mother's house and the door was shut.

Isobel was exhilarated as she wrote her letter. Page after page, she wrote without stopping. Her writing sprawled over the pad, and the sheets piled up on the table. It was as though she had been waiting to write this, waiting for years and years. She didn't even hear the knocking on the front door, she was completely oblivious to it. Until at last, she finished it, and she sat back in the chair in the dining room and closed her eyes and smiled.

That's when she finally did hear the knocking, and also the voices. That's when she got up and went to the front door, and saw all those people. Marion, with that damned frown on her face, holding the girl's hand; the policewoman; the man on the pavement talking to the fat villager, who was saying, 'Yes, that's the girl I saw him with.'

And now here's Sam, striding back up the long, steep lane from the farm which lies down in one of the valleys that are set back from the cliffs.

Look at him! This great, broad-shouldered man with his sandy hair, his massive arms swinging as he climbs the steep hill. The sun is shining well now, the path back at the farm is still and straight and setting hard in the late summer sun, and Sam is marching up the steep lane to go and make himself some lunch at home.

What a sight he is now! He likes this walk, from Bridge's farm back home. He likes the curving, steep lane which winds up past the fields where old Bridge keeps his sheep, and he likes to think of one of those sheep this autumn ending up in the freezer which old Bridge keeps for him.

There are sloe berries along this lane too, and when the crop is good Sam likes to pick these in September to make jam – the same sloe jam his mother used to make and which she used to spread on his bread and have waiting for him when he came back from school. He stops now beside one of the sloe bushes and he reaches up easily to feel the small, fat purple berries that are hanging from the spiky branches.

'That's not bad,' he says to them approvingly. 'That's not bad at all. That could be a good year, better than last year. Not so much rain early summer this year, better crop I think.'

He doesn't taste the berries, because he likes to wait until they are ready before he finds one to assess its flavour and sweetness. No, he carries on up the hill now, which curves around to the left at a fork where another lane leads off into the next valley.

It's about five minutes now before he will reach the top where the lane meets the main road. This is the road that runs along the cliff edge all the way to join the steep hill that leads down into the village.

He likes this walk because the lane is scarcely used and it is always quiet and he likes to feel all the wildlife alive around him inside the tall brambly hedges which line the lane. He knows there are robins' nests in the hedges, because they are noisy, robins, noisy birds for their size. When the females lay eggs the males are noisier than ever, and when Sam hears the male robins calling out protectively he says, 'That's it, you watch over them, you do your job. But there'll be more mouths to feed soon, you'll have your work cut out soon.' And he'll laugh.

He knows that now that summer is drawing to an end

and the evenings are turning colder some of the animals will be preparing for their winter hibernation, and soon the hedgehogs will be burrowing themselves away inside the hedges, covering themselves with rotted down old leaves and earth by the time the cold weather of winter arrives. In the spring he loves to walk up this lane and feel the rustling of awakening inside the tall hedges.

Now the sun is still shining down and he can feel it through the fabric of the shirt on his shoulders. The steep climb has brought out some drops of sweat on his forehead. He likes the fact that this lane is steep enough to bring out the sweat and he enjoys being fit and strong enough still to stride up it cleanly. He knows that in the future, a long time away he hopes, he won't be able to do these things. He knows that when he is old, his life will change, and his routines will have to change to accommodate the failings of his body, but he knows he is strong now and that is a long way off.

He is full of vigour today. His strength is vivid and accurate, and he knows the path he has laid is straight and true. Now he is thinking again of Isobel and how she looked last night, and a broad smile is on his face.

'Ha!' he calls out, and his mood is so buoyant that he does a little skip in one of his great strides, and this makes him remember the girl and dancing on the beach, and he laughs out loud again.

A few paces on there is a gate cut into the hedge on the right hand side, which leads into one of Bridge's fields, and the gate is supported by thick dry stone pillars either side which Sam built four or five years ago. Each one is topped by a heavy flat stone which Sam brought up from the beach below his house, and he puts his thick hand upon one of them now and feels how it is warm from the sun.

He likes to stop here on this walk because he knows there are usually slow worms lying asleep underneath and it amuses him to pick the stone up and to see them. He lifts one of the stones and there are two black snakes asleep on the rock, fleshy black slow worms, and he deftly picks one up with two fingers and for a second it coils in his hand then writhes through his fingers with sudden speed. He lets it drop back onto the rock and he gently lays the flat stone down again.

'You're all right,' he says, and off he is once more, almost at the top of the hill now.

He talks to the wildlife around him, hidden in the hedges.

'Back home now, make some lunch. Isobel should bring the girl back soon, some new clothes. That's good. Sam wouldn't know. Now she'll have some clothes. That's good.'

He has been thinking also this morning while laying out the path that in the Spring he should build onto the house at the back, build another bedroom so that the girl could have her own room.

'Not a difficult job, could easily fit another room at

the back there,' he says now, thinking on it again. 'Would only take me a week, then she'd have her own room then. Nice.'

He would like the girl to have her own room, like his mother did for him when he was a little older than the girl must be now. But things change, and that's all right, it would be good for her to have her own room. And also – and he grins again now as he thinks of this – it would be more correct if the girl was safely tucked up in her own bedroom, and he and Isobel had some privacy.

'I'm flesh and blood, after all,' he explains to the hedgerow. 'She's a nice woman too, she's got a good way about her. Happy about it, very happy about it.' He grins still, and he shakes his head. 'Who'd have thought it though eh? Who'd have thought it?'

And finally he reaches the top of the lane, and look now how triumphantly he stands there at the top! The lane here joins the road which runs along the clifftop, and as he stands with his feet apart and his hands on his hips breathing big clean breaths and with the sweat on his brow, he can see right out over the entire great bay. Right out to where the horizon joins the sea and the sky, all the way from the headland over on the west back to the eastern headland where his house is, although the road is too far back from the cliff edge to see it.

The sun is casting a huge swathe of bright white light over the sea in the middle of the bay, and there are yachts and fishing boats scattered about, and overhead in the clear blue sky a jet plane is leaving a white vapour trail. It is a glorious sight, and Sam stands now with his big chest rising and falling as he settles his breathing after the climb, and he looks out at the view that has stayed constant and ever-changing with him for over fifty years now.

How happy Sam is! A pheasant barks at him as it flies clumsily across the road to settle down in the heather on the cliffs. Sam calls out a greeting and then he sets off once more. He has about a mile to walk before the road begins to descend into the village, and where he turns off for the coast path.

So let's leave him now, Sam. Relaxed and invigorated, walking calmly along the side of the road, his head turned right to view the sea as he walks, his big chest breathing well.

Isobel just can't understand it all. She can't understand what they are all talking about. Why have they made her come back already, they haven't done their shopping yet? Why is she sitting in the back of a police car, driving up the steep hill out of the village? She and the girl are sitting in the back seat, and now the car is pulling up on the left at the top where the cliff path starts. Marion is with them in the back of the car, but Isobel has not listened to her.

Sam won't be happy that she hasn't got the girl's clothes.

Oh, and there he is now! Isobel can see him, striding towards them along the road. The girl has leaped out of the car, and she's running towards Sam. The police-woman calls out something.

Isobel is alone now in the back of the car – all the others are standing in the centre of the road. Sam walks forward quickly and picks up the girl. He sits her on his huge right arm and she nestles her head into his shoulder and her black hair hides her face as it spreads over his neck and shoulder.

'What's this then?' asks Sam quietly. 'What's happened? You all right?'

The policeman who was driving the car walks up to Sam now.

'Excuse me sir, can you please identify this child? Is she your child?'

Sam doesn't know what to do. He has no idea what is happening. He stands still, his big face is frowning, and the girl still hides her head into his neck.

Marion walks up now.

'Sam, who's the girl?' she says.

All Sam can think is that he should get home. This is not right. Not right.

He starts to move forward, and the policeman puts his hand up against his chest, and Sam glares angrily at him, and at Marion, and then he shouts, his voice huge and real up there on the cliff road:

'Get out of my way!'

He is very big, of course, and this shout surprises the policeman. Sam starts to walk with the girl tucked into him, and his face is firm and he is looking diagonally across out to the sea. He is not looking at anyone any more. He is walking towards the start of the cliff path. On his left stands Isobel in the middle of the road. She has got out of the car and she is talking to the police-woman.

Actually Isobel isn't talking to the policewoman, she is just standing there not listening while the woman keeps asking her things. She is looking over towards Sam, then, as though she has heard her for the first time, Isobel turns her head and looks at the woman, and she says:

'I'm going now.'

She runs after Sam, but he is striding forwards and the policeman is following him, shouting questions at him. And Isobel is calling out now, and behind her the policewoman is talking into a radio. Isobel is calling out for Sam, but he is getting further and further away from her.

Sam starts to run now with the girl in his arms down the coastal path and towards the cut-through. He clambers quickly up the steep path of the cut-through, and when he reaches the brow of the hill he stops to catch his breath, and the policeman is not far behind. He calls out:

'Come on Sam, give the girl up! You know you've got to!'

Sam stumbles down the descending part of the cut-through until he reaches the path to his house. When he gets to the gate he lowers the girl gently onto the ground and unlocks the gate, and then he picks me up again and takes me in and we are back in the white washed yard outside of the house.

I stand in the yard and watch Sam shutting and bolting the gate, and then I know what he is going to do, because I've seen it before when I was clearing out one of his aluminium sheds for him.

I can tell what he will do now as I hear the shouts of the policeman who even now is reaching the path to the house from the cut-through. There's nothing I can do about it. Sam is knocking things off the shelves of the aluminium cupboard at the back of the yard, all the things I carefully arranged for him, and then he finds the old shotgun at the back of the cupboard.

I know there are no cartridges in it, and Sam has never fired it – he found it once on the beach years ago, and he kept it because he thought it might be useful one day. And he was right! He's always right.

Poor Sam. He doesn't even see me any more really. He charges over to the wall of the yard and he stands up so he can see over it. He raises the shotgun and points it at the policeman who is now walking down his path.

He yells:

'Get away! Get away! Get away!'

That changes everything of course. The policeman, he

stops, then he steps backwards slowly, and he turns his head and he shouts out:

'He's got a gun! Get back! He's got a gun!'

The people who have followed him – Isobel, the Marion woman, the policewoman – they trip over each other in their panic, which makes me laugh because they look so foolish. I clap my hands, but then they retreat back to the cut-through and hide.

Then everything is suddenly absolutely silent again and I can hear the surf down below on the beach and I look up and see the gulls floating about above us and I wave at them.

Fourteen

Well, it's been very quiet now for a couple of hours. Sam hasn't said anything, and he's been sitting on his bench outside the kitchen where he can see the whole of the bay. He loves that seat. He's got his silly old shotgun beside him, all rusted over from the seawater before he found it.

I'll have to go soon. It's sad; I loved living here with Sam. I loved every single part of it. Sam always said we were a good team, and we were. He used to kneel on the earth in the vegetable garden and pick tomatoes and I would carry them for him. And he let me cut the runner beans myself once, although he held my hand because his gardening knife is very sharp and he was worried that I would cut myself.

I liked making everything tidy for him. He can look after himself, of course he can, but I thought it was nice for him to have his things tidied. He wouldn't have thought of doing it, but I know he liked it. I saw him when he opened the cutlery drawer on the first day I was here and he saw that I had cleaned it out and arranged them all properly, and I know he was pleased.

He told me lots of things. About how the peregrine

falcon spotted the beetles on the cliff, and how to soak the bread for fishing in the can of old fish oil so that it smelled really tasty to the fish. He knows lots more than most people, I think. And now he's sitting there on his bench, and his face hasn't got anything on it now.

Oh, there was a shout then.

It's a man at the end of the path by the cut-through. He looks funny, he's in a suit and he's crouching beside one of the blackberry bushes. He's shouting through one of those loudhailers. He's shouting to Sam, asking if I'm all right, asking Sam to let me out of the front gate. That's just silly, because Sam isn't listening to him, and anyway he's the one they should be asking if he's all right, not me.

Poor Sam.

What's happening out there? Well, soon after Sam got the gun out, lots of people came, some of them are all dressed in black with funny ribbed waistcoats that make them look fat, and they have guns, and they are in different places now around the house. Some of them had to squeeze themselves into positions beside bramble bushes and stinging nettles and they got all scratched and stung and the sun is still hot today so they are all sweaty and uncomfortable. But I think they're used to that, they don't mind it.

Isobel, of course, you know where she is? She's down at the lighthouse now. You know, where she was before, when you go around the back wall of the lighthouse and you can stand overlooking the sea? Well, she's there now. It's about seventy feet from the ledge she's on down to the rocks below, because it's low tide now, so when she jumps off she'll land on the rocks.

She had to give up eventually, you see. When Sam showed the gun and they all ran backwards, she tried to break through to the house and she was crying and crying. The policeman got hold of her, kept telling her she couldn't go to the house, and he dragged her back up the cut-through. She was screaming so loudly. She kept screaming Sam's name.

Then more police arrived and no-one would listen to her. She was still crying, and she tried to explain to them that she had to go and ask Sam's advice. She kept telling them that Sam would know what to do. She said that everything would be all right, but that she had to go and see him. In the end though, they just wouldn't let her move. There was a big policewoman looking after her.

I think Isobel worked out a plan then, because she stopped crying eventually, and wiped her face. The policewoman said 'There, that's better isn't it?' and Isobel smiled at her and said,

'Yes, yes, it's better.'

The policewoman asked if she wanted a cup of tea now, and Isobel said that she did. When she was on her own for a second, she sneaked away from the crowds and ran down the coastal path to the lighthouse. No-one saw her go. Anyway, I think they were all too interested in us.

Isobel is there now, at the lighthouse. She's on her own. Do you know what she's thinking? It's quite funny really. She's thinking about her book. She'll never write it now, will she? But she's been thinking about Héloise and Abelard.

Listen. She's singing now. She's singing part of the chorus that Abelard wrote once. It's supposed to be the nuns who lived with Héloise. She's singing it in a funny voice.

'Let them have respite from their labour,
And from their painful love!
Union for those who dwell in heaven they besought,
Even now are they in sanctuary with the Saviour.'

She's just like that, Isobel. I think she thinks she can see everything clearly now, so that's good. But they'll get down to the lighthouse soon and they'll find her, and then she'll jump off.

The man with the loudhailer keeps on shouting. It is very loud and it echoes all around the yard, and just the noise of it is making Sam mad. He loves to hear the surf from his bench, he loves to concentrate on the noise of the surf, and now this silly man's voice is ruining it.

I think Sam's had enough now.

He jumps up from the bench with an angry yell, a really loud, long, angry yell. He picks up the old shotgun and runs across the yard and leaps up onto the wall and begins to lift the old gun as though he was going to aim it.

Then a bullet is fired by one of the policemen. It spins and spins through the air and I can hear it, whirring like a bumble bee, whirring and spinning through the air. Then there are more of them, and I can hear each one, as they race towards Sam.

And now I am so far up here, up here in the sky, and I can see the bay and the headland and the village, and poor Sam lying there on the concrete by the wall.

Some of the seagulls around me now are starting to swoop down on his house like they used to.

THE END